SHORELINE OF LOVE

SHORELINE OF LOVE

Grace Hamilton

CHIVERS
THORNDIKE

This Large Print book is published by BBC Audiobooks Ltd, Bath, England and by Thorndike Press®, Waterville, Maine, USA.

Published in 2005 in the U.K. by arrangement with Robert Hale Ltd.
Published in 2005 in the U.S. by arrangement with Robert Hale Limited.

U.K. Hardcover ISBN 1–4056–3138–4 (Chivers Large Print)
U.K. Softcover   ISBN 1–4056–3139–2 (Camden Large Print)
U.S. Softcover   ISBN 0–7862–7018–7 (General)

The text of this Large Print edition is unabridged.
Other aspects of the book may vary from the original edition.

Set in 16 pt. New Times Roman.

Printed in Great Britain on acid-free paper.

British Library Cataloguing in Publication Data available

Library of Congress Control Number: 2004110764

CHAPTER ONE

Uncertainty shrouded this expedition as dauntingly as the fine mist which clothed the stormy sea, but of one thing Hope was certain; she could expect nothing but hostility from the islanders when they discovered her purpose.

Sensing the ship change direction, she peered through the porthole window, her gaze skimming past the menacing dark rocks as the ferry turned towards the harbour, bringing her to its bleak destination.

In the distance she could see a small sheltered quayside with half a dozen fishing boats and a scattering of yachts. Following the line of the harbour wall in a gentle curve there were houses encircling the tiny port: no more than a dozen two- and three-storey buildings with faded paint and dullish grey stone walls. Castlebay.

The island's port and focal centre. Little more than a tiny hamlet, gathered around the natural shelter of the rocky inlet like a family surrounding a comforting fire on a winter's night.

Hope groaned. She had been told that Branaigg was a remote island off the west coast of Scotland, but this was worse than even her wildest imaginings. Branaigg was nothing more than a windswept, sparsely populated outcrop of rock which had suffered the misfortune of an oil tanker foundering off its rocky coastline a year ago. She trembled in barely cloaked fear at the thought of spending three weeks alone here, she sensed the inhabitants would be as forbidding as the terrain.

She checked her watch. It was six. By now she would normally be in her flat, running a bath, listening to soothing music, preparing for another Friday night out with Roger. Friday nights they dined together before going on to a club or a party somewhere. Last week the food had been Italian: oodles and oodles of pasta in rich creamy sauces which luckily didn't add an inch to Hope's slim but curvaceous figure.

Living in London, there was hardly a moment in Hope's life that was not filled with one activity or another. If she wasn't out at the theatre or at a club, she was playing squash or swimming. Never a dull moment. Never an empty moment. But now all Hope could do was stare out at her strange new world.

She turned away from the harbour and looked out to sea, resentfully staring at the heavy crashing waves, brooding at the bleak emptiness which the ocean and the two-hour ferry journey had imposed on her. She wanted to go home.

It was all John Davidson's fault that she was here. Life was so unfair.

Hope zipped a paperback into one of the

2

side pockets of her backpack. She had half a mind to leave it on the ferry. It was a science fiction thriller, Roger had chosen it for her; it said something about their relationship that after six months he still had no idea about her taste in novels.

Roger had been disappointed when she had been called away for three weeks. He had been planning to take her to meet his parents in Berkshire. Hope had been relieved to postpone that particular meeting. She realized that Roger was becoming far too serious.

The ferry moved closer to the quayside and Hope picked out several hunched figures huddling against the wind, waiting for the ferry to dock. She wondered which, if any, of the men was Craig McAllister. He wouldn't be expecting her.

She watched as a tall, broad-shouldered, darkly bearded man walked along the quay to join the others. He walked elegantly with long easy strides and Hope found her eyes drawn to him. He joined the assembled group of men and started to talk, and Hope found herself wishing that her binoculars were at hand. For some reason he had taken her interest, distracted her mind from her depressing thoughts, and she would have liked to try to figure out what he was saying.

Perhaps *he* was the enigmatic islander, Craig McAllister, spokesman for the islanders. His name had meant nothing to her until last night. Tired, tense and curiously over-excited, like a child anticipating some strange unknown experience, she had spent much of the train journey trying to make sense of the previous reports, poring over mountains of paperwork as she kept herself sustained with cup after cup of bitter coffee.

His name had recurred again and again in the angry correspondence from the islanders. He had asked for a full environmental survey, but the oil company had only agreed to an independent wildlife survey. Hope's survey. In his latest letter he had informed the oil company that the islanders would not co-operate with the survey. The angry tone of his letter had chilled her to the marrow and she had read and re-read the letter trying to find something pleasant in it. She'd given up in the end. She wasn't looking forward to meeting him. She felt sympathy towards the islanders, but she was likely to get caught in the crossfire between the oil company and the islanders, and one islander in particular; Craig McAllister.

The ferry neared the small quayside. Hope put on her fawn duffel coat and buttoned it up, preparing to brave the Arctic elements. She walked out on to the deck. She could hear the waves crashing against the bow of the ship. A blast of air shot past her face, instantly freezing her features. She plunged her hands deep into her pockets. The wind still whistled

4

about her ears, but Hope vainly refused to pull her hood up, it made her feel too much like a Welsh schoolgirl again, even though it was eight years since she'd left school, since she'd left her roots.

It was hard to believe that she was the same person as the giddy teenager who had tramped through farmland to the Dovey estuary, spending hours alone amongst the mudflats and the sandbars, watching the waders, counting the summer migrants and sketching the softly contoured land. There was a wonderful desolateness about the Dovey estuary with its gentle rhythms and quiet beauty; something in Hope had responded to its natural charm and she had loved being alone in her estuary.

But then she had gone to London, and she had taken to London life like a Welsh duck to water. She lost the feel for aloneness; she lost the feel for bird-watching. Now sometimes she wondered whether she was in danger of losing her roots altogether.

Eyes glazed in troubled thoughts, Hope watched vacantly as a rope was thrown from the ship and caught by a grey-bearded man who took the rope and tied it around the capstan.

She walked back into the lounge. Unclenching her hands, she noted tiny indentations in her skin where her nails had dug into her bloodless palms. Apprehension gripped every cell in her body, resentment following in its wake. She'd never felt like this before. She had been given an impossible job to do.

She heard the ship's engine rumble into a lower gear. Her stomach clenched. She picked up her backpack, numbly slinging it over her shoulder as a cold wave of fear ran over her once more.

She felt half-tempted to stay on the ship. She didn't want to do the job ahead of her, but then again she didn't want to go back to London just now. She knew Roger was becoming far too serious. She liked his company but she wasn't in love with him. He liked to spoil her, but somehow his indulgence always left her with a crawling, sickly feeling in the pit of her stomach. Getting what she wanted never really made Hope happy in the end.

She hesitated as she watched the gangplank lowered. She just wanted to drift. Maybe that's what she was doing anyway? Drifting along on a sea of superficiality pretending that her life was full, pretending she was as happy as people imagined.

As she edged her way down the slippery wooden gangplank in her high-heeled boots, her black velour skirt swirling about in the cold biting wind, Hope looked towards the chilly quayside aware of strange unknown faces staring up at her and felt cold heavy fear again.

With her shoulder length gingery-gold hair, ringletted by the dampness of the sea-voyage into distinctive tight coils of shimmering light, Hope was a natural beacon standing out in the grey fading light of the harbour, attracting attention from deckhands and fishermen alike as she stepped awkwardly off the ferry.

A deep male voice called out from the assembled group of men.

'Bit early for backpacking girlie. Are you sure you've come to the right island?'

She noted a faint ripple of amusement which ran through the assembled men like a Mexican wave at a football game. A herd of wild elephants could hardly have been less welcoming. Her stomach clenched. If this was a normal greeting, how much worse would things get when they found out why she was here?

She looked around to see who it was who had decided to make her the victim of his charming little quip.

A tall, bearded man, eyes as dark as a moonless winter's night stared menacingly at Hope. His hair was a shiny conker-brown, layered and casually flicked from his proud, rugged face. The face was interesting, although by no means conventionally handsome, the nose straight and arrogant, the firm mouth set in a grim line, and now, it was possible to see that the beard which had appeared black from a long distance was in fact a deep mahogany-brown, covering the well-cut shape of his square chin. Now there was no need for lip-reading.

A shiver ran down Hope's spine as she met his steady gaze and noted the cynical half-smile gracing his lips. She looked away quickly, trying to ignore the goosepimples running down her spine, her eyes settling on the mottled grey wet cobbles of the quayside. But the stranger's image burned in her memory. There was something incredibly intimidating about this man, his confident self-possessed stance, his deep dark-eyed stare, his harshly spoken words.

But Hope couldn't afford to feel intimidated. She might be too unnerved as yet to out-stare this dark-eyed stranger, but she had not lost the use of her tongue. Ignoring a wave of fear that ran over her body she took a deep steadying breath.

'I'm not here to backpack,' Hope enunciated as clearly and as calmly as she could, aware of a silly quaver in her voice. She forced herself to meet the stare of those dark shadowy eyes, but there was no reaction, just a dispassionate clinical observation of her pale face framed by its ginger tresses.

'Oh really?' he reacted swiftly. 'My eyes must be failing. I felt sure I spotted a backpack there . . .' He craned his neck to stare at her strident pink backpack.

'Just because I'm carrying a backpack it

8

doesn't mean to say that I'm about to hike all over the island.'

Her antagonist stared coldly at her, his mouth closed to a thin line, eyes dark and forbidding. Something told her this was Craig McAllister. The man most likely to cause her trouble. It looked like trouble had started. He looked about thirty. That was her first mistake about him.

It was cold, the wind was a biting raw screech and the backpack was getting heavier by the second. All Hope wanted to do was get off this cold, dismal quayside and into the warmth, any warmth, and she did not want the unfriendly attentions of any islanders, not now, not ever. She shivered and looked away, avoiding his dark-eyed stare, his alert questioning face coldly exploring her fine-boned features and the pale translucent skin flecked with a small peppering of freckles.

There was silence, broken only by the rhythmic tinkling of the wind running through the rigging of some yacht moored further down the harbour. Hope felt all eyes on her as though the men had been startled by the sound of a woman's voice.

Perhaps they had never heard a Welsh accent before? Her voice even sounded strange to her own ears: she had hardly spoken at all since she had left London; frustration and clawing apprehension had taken her voice away. It seemed that all she had heard for a lifetime were different Scottish dialects and these had simply reinforced her sense of being a stranger in a strange land. Everyone's attention focused on Hope, the hairs on the back of her neck prickled, her whole body fused with a tight unrelenting tension, like an overstrung guitar. She wanted to speak, wanted to break this awful silence, but her throat felt unexpectedly tight and dry, and when she managed to force the words out her voice sounded unnaturally sharp and high.

'Can anyone tell me how to get to the Castle Hotel?'

Once again it was the dark-bearded man who responded to her as though the other men deferred to his powerful presence. 'The Castle? It's not open for business yet. Off-season.'

She knew it was off-season. No one in their right mind would want to make that stormy sea crossing in April, the butt end of winter when many of the worst sea conditions prevailed.

'I *am* expected,' she informed icily.

Hope wasn't entirely sure whether she heard or imagined the faint guffaw of incredulity that preceded the response. 'Are you indeed? I don't believe so.'

Hope detected a cynical knowing tone to his deep resonant voice and she gave him more than a cursory glance. The way he held his dark head spoke of someone well used to authority, the controlled set of his expression

10

and the self-possession in his stance revealed his supreme self-confidence. There was something very impressive about this attractive man.

'I hate to contradict you.' Hope's green eyes flashed a fiery challenge which belied the sweetness of her seemingly benign statement. 'There is a room booked at the Castle Hotel for a Mr. John Davidson, I believe?'

'That's true . . . but,' he paused, a wry smile breaking out across his bearded face, revealing shining white teeth. He turned to the deckhands and then back again to study Hope's intent pale face. 'But you're not trying to tell me that your name is John Davidson? I mean . . . I know we're a long way from the mainland, but we can still tell the difference between a lass and a lad . . . and *you're* no laddie!'

Ripples of unrestrained laughter rang around the dockside, cynical amusement registering on the face of her adversary. She stared numbly at the man. She was angry at him, even more furious with herself for being so slow off the mark in this antagonistic game of words. Was she losing her quick Welsh wits?

A tight dry anger welled up inside her. She hadn't wanted to come to this island, this tiny windswept speck of rock hardly visible on an outstretched map of the British Isles. Yet she had resigned herself to three solitary weeks on the island with nothing for company except

11

puffins, fulmars and gulls.

But now it appeared there was another, even less welcome species for her to contend with: men who loved to belittle women. She took a deep breath and steadied her mind. It was about time she made something abundantly clear. Hope Barraclough was not in the habit of providing free cabaret entertainment for anyone, anywhere—least of all on dreary, freezing quaysides.

'I'm so glad you all find this so amusing.' Hope paused, her sparkling green eyes surveying the cruel laughing faces of the men. She rallied her coldest, severest scientific tone. 'I'm here to carry out the survey. Mr. Davidson was unable to come. I am his replacement.'

The laughter died away to a solemn death, replaced by the stoniest silence that Hope had ever heard. The cruel laughter might have been unpleasant, but this was even more intimidating: the air seemed to crackle with latent animosity. Only the tinkling of the wind through the rigging served to punctuate the silence.

'You had better come with me then. I'm Craig McAllister.'

He stepped oppressively close to her and she felt a twinge of fear at his approach. His body seemed all the more powerful and overwhelming at close quarters. He touched her shoulder, fingering the strap of her heavy backpack. 'I'll take that.'

12

Hope shot a quick glance at his face. It was dark and brooding and there was a contemptuous line to his mouth which sent a shiver down her spine. His hot breath fanned her face, momentarily sending a strange unnerving sensation coursing through her veins, hot breath on frozen cheeks; the first human heat she had encountered on the island.

She slipped the backpack from her shoulder without resistance; something told her that he was used to issuing orders and being obeyed. He could have her backpack. She was, after all, his guest. But she wasn't about to become his compliant little lap-dog.

'Any other luggage?'

His Scottish accent sounded harsh and cold as he barked out his question. His eyes sought Hope's and she flinched at the naked antagonism she saw written across his dark furrowed face.

'A suitcase . . . they took it to the—'

He moved away before Hope was able to finish her faltering, hesitant sentence. She watched as he walked on to the ferry, his long elegant strides taking him swiftly up the gangplank. Hope shivered. Even with her thickest coat on she felt chilled to the bone; goosepimples prickled down her spine whilst gusts of wind swirled her flared black velour skirt up around her legs.

Still, at least she could pull her hood up

again and keep the wind from her head. There was absolutely no one on the island who she wanted to impress with her Pre-Raphaelite flowing ginger locks. How she had hated her hair as a teenager, trying every possible style in an attempt to produce any effect other than curling wild thick ginger locks. By the time she was twenty she had realized that her hair was not for taming, but that given the right cut—plenty of layers and shoulder-length—it flowed and curled in a casual windswept style, her distinctive gingery gold locks framing her fine-boned pale pert face, inevitably drawing appreciative and interested eyes to her like moths to the light.

Until now! Craig McAllister hadn't noticed anything about her, least of all her hair, Hope felt sure of that. She could have walked off the ferry as bald as a coot and he wouldn't have batted an eyelid. She despised him. She wasn't even going to try to get to know the man before she made up her mind about him. Through his letters to the oil company she had formed an impression about him. He seemed to be a bitter antagonistic man. She'd never despised someone on sight before, it was a curious sensation.

'Let's go Miss.'

The air was electric with hostility as Craig McAllister stormed off towards the car-park. Hope almost had to run to keep up with him, struggling in her high-heeled boots over the slippery cobbles. He stopped and turned as he heard the clattering of heels and Hope virtually fell into him. Their bodies brushed. Hope pulled herself rigidly away from his firm, unyielding frame, startled as though she had received some strange electric shock. His narrowed gaze moved from her pale flustered face down over her duffel-coated figure, finishing with a desultory glance at her black leather high-heeled boots.

'I see you came equipped with appropriate footwear.' The voice was scathing, the stare horribly cold, but it was the cynical smile curling his mouth that made Hope want to shudder.

As she met his stare a tide of rage rose inside her. Anger sharpened her features. It emphasized her high cheek-bones, the slight hollows of her cheeks, her mouth, cut like an almost perfect cupid's bow, and the pert uplifted nose, which gave her face a mischievous effect—except when, as now, she was deadly serious.

'I was only given twenty-four hours to prepare for this trip.'

'What happened to your car?'

'Unfortunately it's off the road.'

'Didn't the oil company offer you one?'

'I'm not one of their employees. I'm from the University. This is an independent survey.'

'Independent! I've heard that before.' Bitter cynicism laced his words and Hope had to fight back her fear.

'Look I'm here now. So why don't you get used to the idea? I wasn't aware that I was going to be be frog-marched through the streets of . . .' For a moment Hope's brain seemed to slip a cog. Had the intimidating stare of Craig McAllister scrambled her brain? Or maybe the fog in her head was caused by the cloying exhaustion that had started to seep into every cell of her body. She'd kept going until now on sheer adrenalin alone and now the chemical was all used up.

Whatever the cause, the name of the town slipped beyond her grasp like an ill-remembered name at a crowded party.

'Castlebay?' he responded smugly. 'I suppose it's too much to ask that our visiting environmental scientist should know anything about the island she is visiting—least of all the name of the port she's just docked in.' He paused long enough to look around the harbour in a broad sweep before he confronted Hope once again, dark eyes blazing like flaming arrows.

'You are sure you've come to the right island, aren't you? Maybe you should have gone to Mull, or Lewis, or maybe even the Shetlands . . . possibly they are expecting you in Iceland?'

Hope glanced through heavy lashes, noting the self-satisfied tilt of his brow and the smug line of his mouth, like the cat who swallowed

16

the canary. Anger flowed through every aching cell in her body. Hope looked up briefly into his dark-shadowed face, throwing out her chin defiantly before taking a deep steadying breath.

'Branaigg is an oval-shaped island which measures roughly twelve miles from north to south and eight miles east to west. There is a coastal road which circles the island, a distance of some thirty miles. This, the east coast of the island was most badly affected by the oil spillage.

'Castlebay is the port and largest settlement on the island, with a population of one hundred. To the north there is a township called Traabay centred around the tiny harbour. On the west coast there is a further township called Bernsay, again there is fishing, but also there is farming . . .'

'Everyone farms on this island.' His tone was all-knowing and unimpressed.

Hope stiffened with aloof dignity, she hadn't finished yet and she was not going to be put off course by his ill-timed intervention. She was on home ground here. If there was one thing she could do and do well it was absorb facts: she had read about the geography of the island. Hadn't she tried to use it to get out of coming here? Hadn't she told Marcus Riding, her boss, that it would be impossible to survey the island without a car? Of course Marcus was possessed of a laid-back attitude to life which had been nurtured by the fact that he had never ever wanted for anything in his life. As far as he was concerned problems always resolved themselves. But Hope had the feeling that any problems she encountered on the island were not going to disappear in the twinkling of an eye.

She shot a quick glance at Craig. She was not going to be put off her stride by this over-confident buccaneer of a man.

'Traditionally all islanders have farmed a piece of land, gathered turfs from a particular area and kept animals. However, on the west coast the prevailing Westerly winds provide a softer, gentler climate and the acidity of the soil is ameliorated by wind-blown alkaline shell sand. Consequently, on this coast, there is intensive mixed farming—rye, oats, cattle and sheep above a mere subsistence level.'

Hope looked into his face. She had the feeling he was lost for words. The supercilious smirk had gone, but it had been replaced by a cold expressionless mask which gave away no secrets.

'Very impressive. So the lady has read about the geography of the island.'

Craig ran a slender well formed hand through his hair. Hope noted how well cared for his nails were, his hands were long-fingered but slim; with dark hairs silken on his wrist. A spark of intelligence shot through her brain; perhaps she could win this war of words after

18

all.

'Of course, I believe I made one slight error in my description of the island.'

'Oh really.' Craig looked pleased and more than vaguely interested.

'I did say that everyone on the island farmed, but of course that isn't strictly true is it? I'm sure those hands,' Hope flicked her head casually at Craig, '*never* go near peat bog or cattle byre.'

Craig glared and, without a word turned and started striding out towards the car-park again. He stopped in front of a steel-blue Volvo estate car and turned to her.

'As a matter of interest what happened to Mr. Davidson?'

'He slipped a disc. Or so he says.' Hope snapped out the words. She'd had enough of speaking to Mr. Craig McAllister for one day. She didn't want to be reminded of why she was here, besides, she had the feeling he was weighing her up, cynically making assumptions about her, trying to tease out her weaknesses. She did not trust him.

He lifted one brow in silent amusement. 'Are you suggesting he wasn't particularly keen to come here?'

'Could you blame him? This is hardly paradise.' Hope shivered, the cold biting wind had chilled her thoroughly now. Craig studied the cold, fierce forlorn figure before him, sparkling green eyes flashing life and animosity in the fading light of the quayside.

'Get in then,' he barked out harshly.

His tone was abrupt and unfriendly and she had half a mind to protest at his ignorant manner, but she was cold and dog-tired. She sank heavily into the seat, glad to be out of the biting wind. But Craig didn't start the car. He rested tensed bone-white hands on the steering-wheel and looked out across the harbour.

'For your information your survey isn't what the islanders asked for.'

'You don't say!' Hope spat out the words sarcastically, flashing anger from her vivid green eyes deep into Craig's dark questioning face. 'Don't worry. I got the message. It's hardly a royal welcome I received.'

'What do you expect? There's been a lot of bad feeling since the oil tanker went down last year.'

'You surprise me! So big brawny islanders take it out on unsuspecting environmental scientists who have the misfortune to be sent here. *You* might not be very keen that I am here, but let me tell you . . . I am absolutely sickened to be here. Three weeks watching puffins, counting fulmars and checking off species on this freezing, hostile little island is not my idea of fun.'

It was only when she finished her outraged speech that Hope realized that his eyes were fixed on her, as though he were studying her like a strange specimen under a microscope. She felt her face burn. She turned away, feeling flustered, and in a futile gesture she flung down her hood, flicking her hair out from her collar, tight ringlets cascading out across her shoulders as she turned to stare defiantly out of the windscreen.

She sensed that he was watching her, tiny hairs on the back of her neck prickled with an unfamiliar sensual excitement.

'No. I don't suppose this really is your scene,' Craig drawled, a faint trace of humour in his voice for the first time, and, Hope detected, a tiny echo of Californian years resonant in his voice. She turned her face towards him now, green eyes staring brilliantly into that dark distinctive face. She felt her heart quicken at the intensity of his gaze, but then thankfully his attention strayed from her face as he gave Hope a rather enigmatic full-length gaze.

He started with her Gucci black leather boots, and then his eyes travelled up over her duffel-coated body, noting the finely manicured and highly polished red nails, the tiny gold earrings that adorned her delicate earlobes and finishing when he had fixed her eyes with a stare that emanated from those pools of almost black nothingness.

A trace of a smile crossed his lips and, for once, Hope noted something other than full-frontal antagonism in his eyes: a flash of amusement glinted and she felt she saw the potential for deep dark mischief-making lurking somewhere within the hidden reaches of this mystifying stranger; but then his eyes contracted again and it was as though a cool restraining mask had fallen over his bearded face. Hope sensed that he was weighing her up, fitting together his impressions into a picture of the person he thought she was; for he too would know the lifestyle that she led, he too had lived life in the fast lane, once upon a time.

CHAPTER TWO

A stocky grey-haired fisherman hailed Craig and without a word he stepped out of the car again. Hope shivered at the momentary intake of freezing air, grateful to be left in the comparative shelter of the car. She looked out of the windscreen, her eyes following Craig as he moved with effortless grace, carelessly flicking the shiny conker-brown hair away from his rugged face and listened intently to the fisherman.

Hope looked away, her attention wandering until her gaze settled vaguely on the tiny harbour. She noted how thin patches of light from the houses twinkled on to the choppy grey water; the sheltered port looked almost attractive, a safe haven in a storm. Hope wondered if she could be happy here for a while, if maybe she could enjoy a short respite from her giddy life and the unresolved conflicts which had begun to dog her.

Thoughts of Roger began to spill uncomfortably into her mind. Roger was nice, but if responsiveness was all, then at best she was always lukewarm in his company, never passionate, always self-contained, always aware of the distance between them, aware that she was strangely alone. Sometimes she wondered if she would ever meet anyone who

23

made her head spin or her pulses race . . . it seemed impossible. She frowned and pursed her lips. She needed time to think about her life. Perhaps this could be a retreat, an opportunity to take stock of her life.

She did not notice that Craig had turned towards her, his eyes focused on her pale determined face, noting the tiny frown etching her forehead; her dark brows drawn together in complete concentration.

Hope was still deep in thought when Craig sank back into the driver's seat. He noticed that her face had relaxed, the frown had gone, her beautifully fine-grained skin had become smooth and unfurrowed: she looked dreamy and almost sad.

He spoke out assertively. 'Look. Let's be practical. You don't want to be here and the islanders don't want you here. Why don't I take you back to the booking office . . . the ferry sails with the morning tide?'

Hope felt her heart quicken and her defences rise again. She had thought that hostilities were over for the day, but it appeared there had only been a respite in the battle after all. She fixed Craig McAllister with a challenging gleam, noting in the fading grey light that his face seemed to have taken on a sadder, older hue: there were lines of strain etched on his forehead, lines she had not noticed before. She felt a momentary pang of pity for this dark unfriendly stranger, as though she had just been granted a tiny flash of insight into the complex passionate man by her side.

'I have no intention of leaving this island in the morning.'

Her voice was steady, calm and controlled despite the turmoil blazing inside her. She wasn't aware of the signals streaming out from her alert determined face: the hostile angle of her chin, the slight flush that daubed her chilled cheeks, the blazing green that marked out her darkly fringed eyes.

'I have come here to carry out a survey and I am *not* leaving until I have finished. Do I make myself clear?' She wanted to sound cool and professional, but tiredness underpinned every word she spoke and there was a trembling edge to her final words.

'Are you sure you're up to the job?'

She was shocked at his curt directness. 'Yes. Of course I am,' she answered defensively. His suggestion cut her to the quick. She'd never been less sure of anything in her life but she wasn't about to tell him that. 'Do you want to see my credentials? I was sent here because of my experience. I didn't volunteer.'

Maybe if she'd ranted and raged at Marcus she could have got out of coming here. Marcus wasn't very good at coping with emotional scenes. But something had told her that she had to come here, face her fate and overcome the obstacles before her life could take shape.

His mouth twitched amusedly. 'And how do you propose to get around the island?'

'We'll come to some arrangement.'

'We?'

'Yes. I imagine if I flash enough money around a car will materialize.'

It was a nasty comment to make but she was so exhausted and he was goading her and like a trapped animal she had to claw her way out of danger any way she could. She wished herself back in London, back on familiar territory, away from this desolate island and its hostile people.

Hope glanced into his eyes and then quickly turned away, she hadn't known brown eyes could appear so icy. She shuddered at the disgust which washed across his features.

'People like you think money buys everything.' He spat the words out angrily, and for a fleeting moment Hope had the feeling that he was thinking about someone else.

'People like who?'

'Big city people.'

A nervous half-smile twitched at the corners of her mouth. 'I come from a tiny village in Wales.'

'You might have come from there originally. But you're a big city girl now. From the top of your head to the tips of your toes.' He stopped and glanced at her, his eyes keen and observant and Hope moved her Gucci boots defensively. 'You're probably suffering from culture shock at this very moment. Wishing yourself away from here. Wishing yourself back in London.'

'How dare you!' she countered. He had no right to be so incisive.

'For your information the only reason I am taking you to the hotel is because I can hardly leave you stranded on Castlebay quayside. Money doesn't influence *me* one little bit. I'm more fortunate than my fellow islanders. I'm not a fisherman, consequently I'm not on the breadline.'

'According to the previous surveys the fishing wasn't badly affected by the oil spill.'

'Tell that to the fishermen.'

'Well perhaps I'll find a few things to back up the fishermen's case,' Hope said sympathetically.

'Oh yes?' The caustic retort made colour rush to her cheeks.

'What's *that* supposed to mean?' Hope stammered.

'Well for one, you're only here to study the wildlife . . .'

'And two?' she enquired, feeling totally out of her depth.

'And . . . and,' he drawled, giving her a steady stare as though he were enjoying making her feel uncomfortable, 'you'll produce a report which says exactly what the oil company wants to hear—just like your predecessors.'

A little while ago, standing on the deck of the ship she had been quite prepared to turn tail and run. Now she was staying. She was staying to the bitter end and she knew like she'd never ever known anything before that she was going to produce the most thorough, well-researched report. She would settle this hostility once and for all.

'Is that so?' She'd never felt so insulted in her life. 'I'm independent. I owe allegiance to no one. I will look at the facts thoroughly and I will produce my report. Do you understand?'

'Perfectly.'

She wanted to tell him that she knew all about the island's wildlife, that she had read everything she could lay her hands on about the tidal system, the flora and fauna. But it was pointless. He had closed up like a clam.

There was not a flicker of reaction in the man, the only light that emanated from him came from the glossy dark brown hair that layered shiningly across his well-shaped head. His expression might have been hewn from the same grey impervious stone that marked out his island.

There was a still silence in the car which was broken by Craig's heavy exhalation of breath. He turned the keys in the ignition, flicking on the headlights which flashed their straight unshakeable beam out across the choppy water of the harbour. Craig stared out into that light: the light from her huge green eyes had seemed as strong and unshakeable.

They drove round the harbour in silence and then the car climbed a steep curving hill pulling further and further away from Castlebay. They reached the brow of the hill and began a descent into a lush sheltered valley which was bordered, to the left, by the heavy sea. Hope looked out, almost gasping at the sight before her.

A vast expanse of pure white sand, the whitest sand, the most beautiful beach she had ever seen, a pearly crescent of sand garlanded with black rocky headlands, its beauty was made more poignant by its utter isolation. So this was Traisay Bay. It had escaped the pollution whilst the beaches and shoreline northwards from Castlebay had been thickly coated with the black pungent mess. This bay was simply beautiful and Hope wanted to cry out in delight at the wonder of it all. Instead she bit her lip. She knew that her comments would be misconstrued.

Carefree excitement flooded through her body; for the first time since she had set foot on the island she felt something other than anger, frustration or resentment. All had melted away to be replaced by an awesome acknowledgement of the beauty of the scene before her. She had written off this cold windswept island in the first few minutes, but now Branaigg was unfolding its natural beauty and Hope felt humbled by the desolate power of the scene before her: dark sea, white breakers, black rocks, white sand.

Looking inland, following the yellowed glare of the headlights, Hope could see the tops of trees in a densely wooded copse, and then in amongst the trees she spotted grey turrets and towers. As the road twisted and turned, dropping down into the valley, Hope could make out more and more of the building which lay sheltered in the lea.

It was a vast building which looked out over the bay, stark amongst the encircling trees. It looked like a mediaeval castle and it stood out like an enchanted image from a fairy story with its turrets, angular towers and network of battlements. She had heard that the hotel had been fashioned along the lines of a castle; she had never imagined that the effect would be so magical.

A childlike fascination welled up inside her; she turned towards her silent partner, questions forging themselves in her mind. His face was stern and incredibly intimidating. No. She would ask him nothing.

The car pulled into the car-park, gravel crunching under the car tyres. Craig flicked on the interior light of the car and turned to Hope, car keys jangling in his hand, a faint smirk on his darkly shadowed face.

'I suppose we should be properly introduced. *If* you decide to stay you will have the questionable pleasure of sleeping under the same roof as me for the next few weeks.'

'Don't worry. At university I did field work in the snake-infested rain forests of Indonesia. I can look after myself if I need to.'

Hope was cheered to see that her verbal defiance had washed all the calm arrogance from Craig's face and replaced it with cold stony anger. She was getting some perverted pleasure from goading him into temper. It was little more than he deserved. He started to speak again, only now his voice was as cold and harsh as his expression.

'I gather you know my name. And you are?'

She'd never encountered any man who annoyed her so. But her brain was buzzing in reaction, she was on a roll now as deft as any surfboard rider and facts laced with antagonistic excitement feverishly throbbed through her over-tired brain. There was no stopping her now . . .

'No. Let's hear about you shall we? Craig McAllister. Champion of the islanders. Born and raised on Branaigg until the age of thirteen when you went to school in Edinburgh. Studied English at Cambridge University. Studied Creative Arts and Communication at Berkeley in California and then began a successful career in the film industry. Your career really took off when you directed the hugely successful film "Atlantic Home", the story of a boy brought up in a remote island community. The film won at

Cannes Film Festival and earned you an Academy Award for best director. It was commended for its "startling clarity of vision" and its "evocative and emotive characterization". It was said to be a film from the heart; true, warm, honest and lovingly created.'

Hope spoke quickly and eloquently, the full flow of her words carrying her along as though she were reciting a beautiful, memorable poem, aware all the time that the man beside her was listening avidly, curiously, to every statement she made, his masculine pride bolstered by the sound of his own achievements.

'You returned to the island a year ago, just before the tanker disaster, amid rumours of a personal crisis in your life, although no one has been able to uncover the exact details—'

'That's enough! I can see you've done your homework Miss . . .' His voice was unexpectedly thick, his manner slightly out of control.

Hope cringed. She knew she had gone too far as she watched colour flooding into his cheeks, starkly contrasting with the dark of his beard. Looking up with huge eyes Hope was shocked even further at the rage and sneaking pain that registered in his dark eyes. Suddenly she felt very afraid that he might strike out and hit her, such was the power of the emotions registered in that stranger's face. She knew

32

nothing of the man, how could she know what he might be capable of?

'Miss? What is your name?'

He spat the words out aggressively; Hope felt a further tremor of fear run down her spine. And then she felt annoyed at herself: he was only a man after all, and since when did she allow herself to be browbeaten by such an antagonistic bully? She took a deep calming breath before she spoke again.

'My name is Miss Barraclough.'

'Well Miss Barraclough, let me compliment you on your exceptional memory and ability to ferret out facts.'

But he wasn't being complimentary, and if looks could kill Hope would have expired on the spot: sheer contempt and something else, something frighteningly alien iced his dark hooded eyes. There was a cold merciless pride stamped on his face. His expression was one of cold tight rage and the tension emanating from him caused her heart to pound with heavy hammer blows.

His angry stare seemed to last a lifetime and Hope felt her stomach clench, her pulses race until suddenly, inexplicably, his expression changed and it was as though a mask had been drawn over his face, followed in its wake by the return of chilled, hard self-control. Hope swallowed hard, sensing that there was more he was going to say as she noted the flicker of intelligence that stalked those dark

33

penetrating eyes.

'Can I make a suggestion?' It was a rhetorical question, cynically spoken; his frigid words sent a chill down Hope's spine. 'Confine your investigations to the wildlife of the island. Of course . . . you *may* consider that I belong to that category . . .' His eyes briefly met Hope's before she hurriedly looked away into the encroaching darkness, shuddering at the bitter distaste she had seen etched on his face.

'I . . . I . . .' She hadn't needed to spew out all that speculation about his personal life. But it was a sad fact that she never knew when to stop, she never knew when to keep her big mouth shut.

'I would be very grateful if you could keep your pretty little nose out of my personal life.'

Hope blushed at that, red-hot heat surging into her cheeks. She felt thrown off balance by his personal remark about her nose, people always noticed her cheeky little nose, and somehow, in the midst of all this baiting, he, Craig McAllister, had stopped long enough to notice her, maybe not as a woman, but at least as another member of the human race. And now, for the first time, shockingly, inexplicably, Hope became aware of the maleness, the latent virility of the man beside her and it frightened her.

'I'm sorry . . . I shouldn't have commented on your personal life, I—'

'No you shouldn't . . . little Miss

Environmental Scientist.'

The arrogant self-righteous tone of his words fused every nerve ending in Hope's body into outraged frustration. Why had she apologized? Craig McAllister had twisted her apology. He wanted to make her squirm. This man didn't appreciate apologies, just total submission to him, the indomitable male. He only recognized victory and defeat; and defeat was something he had obviously never grown used to.

Craig stepped out of the car and retrieved Hope's bags from the boot. Hope stood up and looked at him. He was studying the monogram on her case. He looked up and gave Hope a cold icy stare before he spoke.

'"H"? What does the H stand for? Let me guess . . . Hecate . . . Greek goddess associated with witchcraft and magic? . . . Or possibly Hecuba, killer of King Polymestor and his sons? . . . Or maybe Helen? undoubtably one of the most dangerous and most beautiful of women, cause of the Trojan War? . . . am I getting warmer?'

Why did he have to continue to be so nasty to her? It wasn't even a heated aggression, it was a cold, soulless war of attrition, a demoralizing continual baiting. Hope wanted it to stop, but she wasn't going to let Craig know that she suddenly felt fragile, punchdrunk, beyond words. Maybe it was just tiredness. After all, she had been travelling for

35

the best part of two days. Or perhaps it was hunger; the last thing she had eaten was that curled-up cheese sandwich early in the morning. Whatever it was Hope wanted out: out of the cold, out of the war zone and out of the company of this confrontational male.

'The name is Hope.'

'Hope.'

He turned the word slowly around his mouth as though savouring a fine wine, or some new exotic tropical fruit. 'How appropriate.'

Hope lifted big green eyes to stare unfalteringly at him, but a traitorous blush spread over her cheeks, giving a lie to her resolution. She prayed that her colour would go unnoticed in the dim grey light.

She wanted to stay a stranger to him. He was her enemy. Would he have been as antagonistic towards John Davidson or did he save his real contempt for women alone? Hope could only guess, but about one thing she was certain—Craig McAllister would seek out her weaknesses, for he was predatory and she had obviously been marked out as prey.

She shivered, hearing the softened sound of the wind swirling through the trees of the valley, the eerie note of a lone owl hooting mockingly somewhere out in the depths of the darkness.

'Go in out of the cold.' His voice had an unexpected gentleness to it and Hope

36

trembled.

Craig indicated the vast double oak doors of the hotel with their round black wrought-iron handles. She approached the doors, stepping awkwardly through the loose gravel in her high-heeled boots. She turned a handle and pushed the heavy creaking door open. She hesitated now, on the threshold of her temporary home, as though afraid to go in, afraid to enter the lion's den.

Suddenly she sensed Craig behind her, she felt his eyes on her back, making the skin on the back of her neck prickle again in that curious way. His warm breath fanned her cool cheek as he whispered softly in her ear.

'It's safe to go in. It's not true what they say— we don't eat mainlanders for breakfast any more.'

The proximity of his body sent a flood of heat coursing through her frame. His chest was against her back, it felt hard and muscular, unrelenting power and strength seemed to suffuse every sinew of his body. She shouldn't have turned round then and looked up into his face. But she was impulsive. Act now, regret later. It had always been her motto.

The man she saw before her now was very different to the antagonistic adversary who had baited her since she set foot on the island. The light from the hotel lobby was thrown directly on to his face. His skin was pale, almost bloodless under the scrutinizing light, his dark brows no longer seemed the threatening boundary to deep brown piercing eyes, for now there was a hint of warmth and humour lurking within those powerful orbits. His mouth was relaxed and slightly open, the male lips proudly offset by the dark heavy beard that was clipped neatly around the elegant contours of his face. His aggression had dissipated.

All Hope saw now was a dark attractive man with quick observant eyes, and yet, there was something else. Faint lines of strain etched his features, dark shadows lurked under his eyes, and there was something as yet unreadable in those eyes, but it was something she did not fear. For a fleeting moment Craig had stripped away the pretensions, the antagonisms, the cold war. For a brief moment he allowed her to see the vulnerable human being beneath the prickly aggressive façade. Hope felt her heartstrings pull, a soft warm feeling blossomed inside her in a way she had never experienced before.

She did not, could not, understand all that she had seen there and instinctively she knew that this dark troubled man would close up against her almost instantaneously, denying with a cold haughty mask that he had ever reached out, ever sought contact with the young interloper who stood before him.

He looked away, and Hope moved into the stark light of the lobby. She felt puzzled at the strange unnamed feeling that had coursed through her, but then, flushing it out of her mind, she took a deep steadying breath and reminded herself that she was a scientist. Craig McAllister was a mystery to her. She needed to know more about him. She wanted to know how best to handle him. Who was he? He wasn't just the simple islander he affected to be in his heavy cable jumper, well-worn cords and dark beard. Nor was he a slick, sophisticated Hollywood director. What made Craig McAllister tick? Hope told herself her concern was purely in the interests of science, as she pushed aside the thought that she had no recollection of ever having been so acutely aware of another member of the opposite sex.

CHAPTER THREE

Hope found herself face to face with a roomful of dull glazed eyes, all peering down from the high walls of the lobby—deer, fox, stoat, hare, all bore lasting witness to the skills of taxidermy with their sad fixed expressions and dull coats of fur. Hope shuddered and shot a fierce glance at Craig.

'I know what you're thinking little Miss Know-it-all, but I plead not guilty. These came with the hotel.'

'Couldn't you get rid of them? It's so awful to see them arranged like trophies.'

'Oh! I see. I put them out in the old barn, to save your delicate sensibilities? It won't bring them back again you know. At least when people see the animals here, it makes them realize we have to protect wildlife— something that no one gave much thought to a hundred years ago. There aren't any of those about any more,' Craig indicated a snowy-tailed rabbit which was perched docilely in the corner. 'They died out fifty years ago.'

'Who did all the hunting?'

'A man called John Postlethwaite. He was a businessman from Yorkshire who made his money in wool. He built this whole place as a hunting lodge. A bizarre sort of sporting palace for him and his friends. He even imported deer to build up a stock to shoot. He died in 1932 and his son took over ownership. He was killed in North Africa during the Second World War and the whole place fell into disrepair.' Craig spoke without aggression, no more the cutting edge to his California-softened Scottish accent, and Hope felt herself relax, wondering whether Craig realized he was actually talking pleasantly to her for once. 'No one else in his family wanted to be bothered with the estate. It looked as though it was going to have to be demolished—'

'And then you stepped in . . .' Hope added bouncily, a trace of mock cynicism on her lips.

There was a pause, a stony empty pause and silence. Only silence on Branaigg was like no other silence Hope had ever encountered. Always, always it was accompanied by a deep undercurrent of hostility. And this time it was all her own fault. Why hadn't she kept her big mouth shut? Now Craig would never open up again. He had actually been talking to her normally. But that was all over now. Hope could see the storm clouds brewing; the furrowed dark brow, the tight compressed lips, the venomous glare from the dark penetrating eyes. Her silly cocky remark had changed the whole atmosphere irretrievably. Craig spoke and ice-cold anger splintered out along with his words.

'But of course I'm forgetting. You already

know it all. It must be in your well-remembered research somewhere. All about this place. All about me.'

Hope felt her stomach clench. Her nerves shattered into thousands upon thousands of tiny threads. At that moment she would have given the world to recapture that peaceable calm which had eased its way between them for those few fleeting moments. She glanced briefly at Craig. He looked stern and forbidding, her stomach churned anew, but she didn't want to give in to her inexplicable fear. Maybe it wasn't too late to retrieve the situation, perhaps a few well chosen words would make him understand.

'No . . . no . . . I don't know all about you . . . or the hotel.'

Now he gave her a cold churlish stare, as though he was hardly listening to a word she said. Turning his back on her, he called out into the emptiness of the building.

'Mrs. McClennan!'

Almost immediately a short plumpish woman in her early sixties shuffled along the hallway, her feet encased in fur-lined woollen slippers. Greying hair was pulled back tautly from her broad face into a furled knot and she was dressed in a thick brown woollen shift which was partially covered by a huge starched white cotton apron.

'This is Miss Barraclough. She's here instead of the Mr. Davidson.'

42

Vacant oblique hostility filled the housekeeper's face like the unspoken antagonism Hope had sensed from the islanders on the quayside.

'I'd better be showing you to your room then lassie . . . though what a girl like you wants to be . . .' The rest of her words were lost in a monotonous mumble as Mrs. McClennan trudged heavily back along the hallway.

Hope stepped quickly along the high-ceilinged corridor. The walls were festooned with typical Scottish prints—lochs, mountains, cattle in those particular hues of grey, brown and green so beloved of the Scottish landscape artists of the nineteenth century.

As she slipped noiselessly through the richly carpeted splendour of the hotel Hope smelt the unfamiliar aroma of home cooking. Not the overpowering foody smell of a restaurant, nor the half-hearted effect produced by microwave dinners, frozen pizzas or take-away food. This was the real thing. It was normally only when she went home to Wales that she smelt that warm comforting aroma. It seemed to mix in with all the other essences—freshly cut flowers, highly polished furniture, newly laundered clothes—and give a warm comforting atmosphere to a house. But Hope was a long way from home now and her heart sank anew when she contrasted the warmth and love of her Welsh family to these bleak

43

unwelcoming islanders.

She followed Mrs. McClennan up a vast curving, dark wooden staircase, dogging her steps until the woman stopped outside a room marked with a wrought-iron number two. Unceremoniously the housekeeper flung the door open, revealing a small single bedded room. It was an attractive enough room, but Hope was disappointed. She needed somewhere to work. There would be maps and charts and reams of results. Organizing and writing up was going to be difficult in this room. Mrs. McClennan flounced silently away before Hope had a chance to say anything.

She walked over to the window, her spirits flagging. It seemed to be one problem after another. She pressed her nose up against the cold window pane. In the dark distance she could just make out white breakers. She gasped with joy. There was an uninterrupted view of her beautiful bay. This made up for everything. She rubbed the condensation from the window and peered intently out into the darkness, feasting on the dark shadowy land beyond.

'It's so beautiful here . . . I've just never ever seen a more wonderful place in my whole life . . .' Hope murmured, her voice a spirited whisper.

She turned then, away from the black waves with their white-tipped tops, away from the dark shadowy rocks looking back into the bright light of the room. She had thought she was alone, but Craig McAllister stood before her now. Tall, powerful and incredibly attractive, his dark hair flicked off his face, he stood in silence, his deep brown eyes locked in renewed assessment of the fiery petite young woman who stood framed in the window, bright glowing energy and joy shining out from her pert, pale face and her flowing ginger tresses.

'Oh . . . I didn't realize—' The words died on her lips. He watched as the uninhibited animation drained from her face, like air leaking out of a punctured balloon. His searching gaze lingered on her face for a moment, absorbing the flush of pink that rose in her soft shapely cheeks, his keen intelligence aware of the embarrassment she felt at discovering she had been overheard by him.

'Will this room suit?'

He had a sort of smirk on his face and Hope had the distinct feeling that having caught her with her guard down he now felt he had an advantage over her.

'I was hoping for somewhere to work.'

The smirk disappeared and a chilled expression took its place. 'No one said anything to me about it.'

'Well I'm saying something now!' she quipped nervously.

He stared obliquely at her for several

seconds and Hope squirmed under his mocking appraisal. She was in his power. He could make her life as uncomfortable as he liked, and when a half-smile appeared on his lips Hope knew what it was to be a fish struggling on a line.

He turned and started to move off, hesitating in the doorway, his eyes contracted to dark slits. Somehow she knew the subject was closed even before he opened his mouth.

'Perhaps you can find your way down to the dining-room when you are ready? . . . Naturally, I would imagine that someone who has successfully navigated the rain-forests of Indonesia should be able to orienteer her way to the dining-room without an escort.'

He was gone before she had a chance to respond. Life with Craig McAllister was going to be nothing but trouble. Perhaps things would get easier once she had the survey on the go. If she was busy, moving around the island, she could be free of him. He was an annoyance. He had obviously decided to make her task as difficult as he could.

Alone inside the cosy warm bedroom Hope threw off her heavy duffle coat and slumped exhaustedly on the soft bed. She looked around the room, pleasantly surprised at the stylish and well co-ordinated decor; walls papered with a fine floral French blue print, and the shade picked up again in the plain blue satin eiderdown and velvet curtains, whilst the thick pile carpet was a motley combination of creamy hues. Maybe there was a Mrs. McAllister after all, for this room showed a woman's touch, and somehow Mrs. McClennan didn't look the artistic type.

As Hope lay back, her head nestling in the soft pillow, she could not hear a sound. How different from the noisy street clamour that she was used to. She wondered whether Roger was eating out alone tonight and then, all too easily she dismissed him from her mind. She pulled herself up from the comfort of the bed and sought out the bathroom, wondering what her face looked like after the ravages of windswept Castlebay.

Hope groaned as she caught sight of her face in the mirror. Her hair was wildly wind-blown about her shoulders, her pale skin almost translucent under the glare of the light, whilst her curvaceous red lips and her large green eyes seemed to stand out vividly on her strained face. There were grey shadows under her eyes, and, not for the first time, she began to wonder whether she was up to the struggle in front of her. The survey was going to be difficult to do anyway, without animosity from the islanders, and one lovely beach to look out on to wasn't going to alter that reality one iota.

She pulled a brush through her hair ruefully wishing that she was back in London; back with her friends; back on home territory; back where she could relax. Right now she felt as though her nerves were all tuned to their highest pitch. This was all so new, all so different, and it was all going to be so difficult.

She still didn't know how she was going to get around the island. She had nowhere to work and the natives weren't exactly friendly. Handling Craig McAllister was turning out to be more problematic than dealing with a swarm of bees. She would have to tackle him again over dinner. There was no other alternative. She fixed her lipstick and flicked mascara on her lashes, noting the sparkling light of battle that gleamed in her wide green eyes. Tonight when they dined she would have to try charm and feminine wiles with the enigmatic Craig McAllister.

The vast dining-room was totally empty, a few lights illuminating the far corner of the room where a small solitary table was laid. Hope wandered towards her place, pushing thoughts of London Friday nights firmly out of her mind. It was only as she sat down that she realized the table was only set for one.

CHAPTER FOUR

The following morning when Hope woke, blue-hued light was filtering into the bedroom through the curtains. The world was silent, save for occasional bird-song. She checked her watch. It was after eight. She'd slept for ten hours. She must have fallen asleep as soon as her head hit the pillow. But now the events of the previous twenty-four hours flooded into focus and Hope cringed at the memories. Last night's solitary meal burned afresh in her mind. She had assumed mistakenly that they would eat together but Craig had been noticeable only by his absence. Consequently, she hadn't been able to settle the problem of transport or working space.

She had half a mind to disappear under the covers and conveniently hibernate for the next three weeks! But then she remembered the one ray of sunshine she had encountered. She threw back the covers and sped to the window. The bay. It was still there! Hurriedly Hope washed and dressed, throwing on thick navy cords, a blue checked fleecy cotton shirt and a thick Shetland wool jumper flecked with blue and grey. Out came the heavy brown leather walking shoes—a rogue cobweb still clinging to one of the laces.

There was no sign of anyone as Hope

trundled heavily into the dining-room. She called out, but since there was no response she decided to wander outside. She scrunched purposefully through the empty car-park imagining, for a brief moment, that she was the only person on the island.

Perhaps she should go off on a reconnoitre; enjoy her freedom for the moment, since Craig McAllister, her self-appointed shadow, seemed to have disappeared with the night. Hurriedly Hope collected her coat and started to stomp up the hill towards Castlebay. Having reached the top of the hill, she had a panoramic view of the island. There were few other high points on Branaigg and Hope had an unrestricted view of the north-easterly coast with its rugged rocky inlets and soft sheltered bays. Looking down into Castlebay, Hope could make out tiny figures scurrying around the dockside; fishermen hard at work.

Hope's stomach started to rumble. She should head back to the hotel and try to rustle up some food. But no. Perched on the top of the hill here, it was just as easy to tramp down into Castlebay. Free of Craig McAllister, this would be a perfect opportunity to speak to the fishermen.

As she rounded the curve of the quayside, the wind seemed to swerve around like a vortex, picking up speed, whipping up rigging and sending shivers through Hope's delicate frame. She approached the fishermen; some

50

men were loading empty boxes on to a boat, whilst another man sat on the quayside unravelling nets. He looked up briefly, and then turned away without acknowledging her, continuing his work. She recognized him as the man who had spoken to Craig the night before.

'Good-morning.' Hope's greeting was to no one in particular, but it may as well have been to the wind, for no one responded.

She repeated her greeting, this time at greater volume, an uneasy feeling welling up in her stomach. 'Good-morning.'

Still there was no response. Hope felt her heartbeat quicken anxiously. She suddenly felt intimidated, her good humour at walking alone on this desolate but beautiful island had all dissolved. Once again she knew that passive hostility towards her was the order of the day; but Hope was not going to be beaten by the silent fishermen.

This time her strident Welsh tone sang out over the windy quayside. She didn't care if the whole of Castlebay heard what she had to say! 'Where I come from it's good manners to acknowledge someone's greeting.'

The men stopped at this. Stopped and stared icily at the newcomer, her gingery hair spilling out from her hood, her face fixed in a determined stare. She stood there. Tiny, duffel-coated, her hands flung belligerently in her pockets, her chin tilted upwards in defiance. Twenty-four hours ago their intimidatory gaze would have shocked her, but Hope had seen it all before and now she found she had half anticipated their response.

'Well maybe you should be getting back there.' It was the man nearest to her who spoke. He dropped the nets, planting his hands defiantly on his hips. He was short and stocky, with thick grey hair. He looked about the same age as her father, though there was nothing remotely paternal in his attitude! A momentary tinge of fear ran through her at the intimidatory tone of the fisherman, but it was soon overridden by anger. Pure white anger.

'Is this the way you treat all newcomers to this island? Or did you reserve this greeting especially for me? . . . I can't say I've been struck by friendliness since I landed here.'

'Look.' The tone was softer now and when the fisherman looked at Hope he seemed as though he was looking at her for the first time. 'You've not come here to make friends have you? You're here for the oil company.'

'I wanted to ask you how the pollution has affected your fishing.'

'Read the reports. According to them the fishing hasn't been "significantly affected". And what difference does it make to you? You're not here to study the fishing.'

'Who says?'

'Craig McAllister. You're here to count birds, aren't you?'

Everywhere she went Craig McAllister haunted her. He had stamped his mark on every person and she couldn't escape the suffocating feeling that his antagonistic attitude to her would close every door, block every channel on this island. There was nothing but hostility wherever she went. Her heart sank, a twinge of fear ran through her blood, coldly. She didn't know if she could face this continual struggle alone.

Everything centred on Craig McAllister. If she could convince him that she was honest and impartial . . . and less threatening than the great white shark. And yet . . . the man irked her so a moment in his company sent her hackles rising; he was the last person she wanted to try to ingratiate herself with.

Fixing her eyes on the scavenging gulls that squawked and shrieked in their fight for fish scraps she trudged slowly up the hill and out of the little town. She was tired, hungry and dispirited. Overhead she noticed dark stormy clouds.

Before she had reached the brow of the hill rain started to fall. It pelted against her, cold, penetrating, and as hostile as everything else she had encountered on the island. Within a few moments Hope was drenched through. She hurtled the last few hundred yards to the hotel, noticing that Craig's car was now parked in the front. She flew in the door, and stood on the mat—dripping; shivers shaking her chilled,

53

hungry, despairing frame.

Her entry did not go unnoticed. The dark figure of Craig appeared along the hallway. Hope tensed. He was the last person she wanted to see now. Especially as she felt more like a drowned rat than the cool environmental scientist she was affecting to be.

'Good-morning.' There was a mocking tone to his voice and, as Hope threw him a sharp-eyed glance she noted a derisive smile twisting his lips.

'Is it?' she snapped, suddenly recalling the full belt of the fishermen's churlishness and wanting to off-load her frustration right back on him. But then he probably wouldn't even notice it. He was far too thick-skinned and arrogant to be affected by any venom she might spit at him.

'Oh dear. Has a spot of rain dampened our little scientist's enthusiasm?'

Little scientist indeed! Since when did size have anything to do with competence? Hope decided to ignore that particularly puerile remark and was about to comment that his spot of rain was more like a deluge. But she held her tongue. Why should she give him the benefit of knowing that there was nothing she hated more than getting sopping wet?

'Or perhaps we didn't sleep very well last night?' Craig taunted in a mock-sensitive tone, tilting his head to one side, letting his eyes linger on the tiny bedraggled figure before

54

him. He paused deliberately and then smiled slowly as his eyes returned to her waiting stormy face.

She drew a hand over her face, wiping the rain from her flushed cheeks, flicking her bedraggled ringlets over her shoulder.

'I slept very well thank you. My problem is not sleeping, but the nightmare I wake up to. I walked down to the quayside. I decided to speak to the fishermen . . .' At this Craig's eyebrows rose and his smile broadened, only it was the cruellest coldest smile Hope had ever witnessed.

'Don't tell me . . . let me guess . . . you weren't exactly made to feel . . . welcome?'

'Well done! Got it in one.' Blind fury fuelled Hope's movements as she started to unbutton her wet, heavy coat, aware of tiny cold drops of rain seeping down the back of her shirt. 'But then I would expect you to know how the fishermen feel since you've fuelled all the animosity towards me. You're responsible for all this bad feeling: you and you alone.'

Hope's cheeks flamed hot and her eyes flashed brief and brilliant. Maybe she had said too much, but she felt better now, she had exorcised the frustration she felt towards him as effectively as a primal scream. She shook the random drops of rain from her coat, like a dog shaking out its fur, and then she started to stride arrogantly past Craig, her chin defiantly raised.

55

'Not so fast.' Craig's strong firm hand grasped her arm, pinning her close to him. So close she could pick up that same clean masculine smell she had detected on him last night. So close that his cream cable jumper was dampened by her coat—that alone gave her a bittersweet sense of satisfaction, pinned as she was by this overpowering masculine aggression. Hope forced herself to meet his dark penetrating eyes, but then she almost flinched from the glittering fury she saw in them. He started to speak, the words snapped out of his grimly held mouth like bullets from a gun. 'For your information I am not . . .' at this, Craig tightened his grip on her arm and brought his dark bearded face down close to hers. She could smell coffee on his warm breath, hear the slightly ragged quality of his breathing and, when he started to speak again, she sensed the whiplash-tight control of his anger. 'I am not the cause of any bad feeling towards you, Miss Barraclough.'

He frightened her. She trembled and then took a deep breath. She couldn't afford to let him know how terrified she felt.

'Oh. How formal we are this morning.' Now it was her turn to be sarcastic. 'Perhaps you can explain to me why everyone treats me as if I've got a particularly virulent strain of the plague.'

'I told you.' His eyes bore into her, words spilled quietly, coldly from his intimidating

56

face. 'Everyone is bitter over the treatment they have had from the oil company.'

'It's not just that though, is it? You fuelled the fire. You told the fishermen that I wouldn't be looking into their problems.'

'It's true though isn't it? You're not here to look into the problems of the fishermen, are you Miss Barraclough?' As he spoke, cynicism iced his eyes in a horribly chilling manner, sending a solitary shiver coursing down Hope's spine.

She stared remotely into those forbidding eyes, bluffing wildly that she felt as cool, calm and collected as her adversary. Aware that her stomach was churning in the most alarming manner.

'You make it sound as though you know more about my intentions than I do.'

'I probably do—you told me yourself that you only had twenty four hours' notice. I've been on this issue for over twelve months now. I'd say that gives me a headstart.'

'Maybe you should brief me on what you know. Share your knowledge. It might help me.'

'I don't think you need any help from me,' he responded cynically.

'What do you mean by that?' Hope stammered, hating the undertone in his voice.

'I mean—'

'Mr. McAllister! There's a phone call for you . . .' Mrs. McClennan hurried along the

57

corridor. Hope stared at Craig who raised a brow.

'Looks like we'll have to finish this conversation later,' he drawled with a cruelly cynical smile on his dark attractive face.

CHAPTER FIVE

It rained incessantly throughout the day and Hope was ensnared by the weather, forced to stay in, reading and re-reading the dreaded reports which she had lugged all the way from London. More than anything she now wanted to extend the remit of the survey. Merely focusing on the bird and wild animal population when there was so much unresolved hostility over fishing seemed ludicrous. The fishermen claimed their catches were down, although the previous surveys had found that all the fish were healthy. The arguments seemed unending. Perhaps there was a way to settle the problem . . . her thoughts returned to the recent research on mussels . . . maybe . . . but she couldn't be sure . . . she would have to keep all her ideas to herself.

After another solitary dinner Hope returned to her room. She looked out of the bedroom window. The rain had ceased and it seemed as though the wind had dropped. It was dark outside, but the light from the moon lightened the silvery sand of the bay in an almost ghostly manner. Now was the time to walk out to her bay. There was not a moment to lose. The unyielding scrunch of gravel underfoot was replaced by the soft, springy, silent sensation of tussocky grass. After fifty yards or so, the soft bouncy grass with its hummocky mounds and rabbit warrens gave way to a sandy path which was marked out on either side by tall coarse marron grass. When Hope reached the end of the path she found she was at the top of a sand dune which drifted down into the main body of the crescent-shaped bay: a bay which was garlanded at either end by headlands of rugged dark rocks. The sight of the beautiful deserted bay made Hope feel ecstatic, fresh and new. She was free to listen to the gentle lapping of the waves on the seashore and watch the moonlight on the undulating water. Suddenly it all seemed wonderful and her heart filled with joy.

Down, down through the cloying, ever moving dry sand Hope slipped through the dune, aware of sand seeping into her shoes. She stopped briefly when she reached the hard white sand of the beach, but then she took off for the water's edge, embraced by a childlike desire to get to the water, feeling like a schoolgirl at the seaside once more.

Waves no more than a foot high broke on the shore lapping gently to a tiny trickle on the wet sand and Hope felt an unquenchable desire to paddle. The water would be freezing. She had no towel, but what did it matter? Impulsively she threw off her shoes and socks, rolled up her trouser legs, exposing her legs and feet to the chill Scottish air. This was crazy! She let out a yelp of excitement as she paddled into the water. A tiny tail of a wave washed over her feet and Hope jumped at the chill that tickled through her feet.

Within a few minutes her feet and shins were totally immersed in the freezing water. She paddled along the beach, swishing through the water and leaping through the tiny waves which broke on the shore. Pure joy ran through her body and she wondered if she could really and truly be the same person who had pined for parties and nightlife last night. When was the last time she had felt as free as this?

The moon dipped behind a cloud and the wind began to chill her face. Her toes were going numb and she ran back to her shoes, picking them up and tying them together by their laces before she hurried back with them towards the dunes. Hope picked her way gingerly along the path, at first feeling the sand hard beneath her feet and then the soft tickly grass as she moved in the total darkness towards the gentle lights of the hotel. Suddenly a dark shape loomed up ahead of her. Shocked and frightened, she let out a startled gasp, shuddering at the tall shadowy figure before her, dropping her shoes so that they landed with a dull thud on the grass.

'What the devil do you think you are doing out here?' In the faint light thrown out by the hotel lights, Hope noticed that Craig's hair was wind-tousled, his brows joined in a tight furrow, his eyes seeming like black dots of nothingness sunk into their sockets.

'I . . . I came out here for a walk,' Hope faltered, her heart beating in strong hard strokes, her pulses almost audible.

'You shouldn't have come out here on your own.' His tone was both patronizing and condescending.

The first wave of shock receded and Hope found that it was superseded by anger: anger that he was deigning to speak to her as though she were a silly little girl. All her senses were on red alert as she began to speak.

'As I tried to explain to you before, I am quite capable of looking after myself. And, despite the verbal animosity towards me, I hardly imagine I am going to be the victim of an assault on this island.'

'You left the hotel without letting anyone know where you were going.' Now there was a quiet control to Craig's voice. His tone was arrogant, as though he knew he was on the winning side in this argument. 'I've looked all over the hotel for you and I find you wandering about in the pitch dark.' At this he lowered his gaze, and in the dim light thrown out from the hotel he was able to make out Hope's bare legs and feet. 'What on earth have you been doing?'

'I've been paddling.' It sounded so ridiculous now, she felt like a silly child, but

62

annoyed too that Craig made her feel so belittled.

'Paddling? In this weather? Are you crazy, woman? The sea is absolutely freezing.'

'I know,' Hope offered quietly.

'What kind of crazy fool are you? Don't you realize that it's very easy to have an accident out here in the dark? You might have slipped on the rocks. Or in amongst all this coarse grass with its rabbit warrens. It's very easy to sprain your ankle—or break a leg. You could have been out there all night in the cold, developing hypothermia.'

'I'm sorry, I didn't think.' As soon as the apology crossed her lips Hope regretted it. She remembered how he'd jumped on her previous apology. No doubt he was about to give her chapter and verse on island safety for good measure.

'No. You didn't think did you?'

Why couldn't he just accept her apology and leave it at that? He just had to rub her nose in it didn't he? His stormy voice cut across Hope's angry thoughts.

'But of course you are right about one thing.' There was a cynical tone to his voice now, and Hope didn't like it one little bit. 'There is no crime on this island so you are hardly likely to be the victim of an assault. I can assure you that you will leave this island without as much as a hair on your head being touched . . . and with whatever modesty you

63

possess still intact.'

That last remark was just one remark too many for Hope. Her modesty, as he so delicately put it, was all hers. She slept alone. Had always slept alone. Her relationships with men had never developed further than a few chaste kisses. She had never wanted anything more than that. She was scared of her emotions, scared of involvement and, moreover, she had never met anyone who had stirred her feelings warmer than luke-warm. And here was this stranger jumping to all kinds of conclusions.

It was too much. Red-hot fury leapt through her and without a thought she lashed out and swiped him across the face. Shock ran through her as she realized what she had done, and then she found that she had been manacled by two strong hands which easily boundaried her slim wrists. His grasp was hard and unrelenting. Hope struggled to free herself.

'Let me go,' she hissed angrily, wincing with the pain. She had imagined his slim long-fingered hands to be weak and effete, but now she had plenty of time to discover how powerful they were. Struggling was useless, he merely tightened his hold on her, his warm hands burning against her chilled slim wrists.

'You're quite a little vixen, aren't you, foxy lady?'

'Let me go!' A fiery sense of righteousness burned up her spine.

'No. You'll probably hit me again. Though why you hit me in the first place is quite a mystery to me.'

'Oh. Is it now? If I have to spell it out . . . and I suppose I should expect that an arrogant, aggressive man such as you would be blind to any offence he might have caused . . . As it happens,' Hope continued, her voice as haughtily Welsh as she could manage, 'I took exception to your remarks about my "modesty". For your information . . .'

Hope stopped talking. He had loosened his grip on her hands slightly. Craig McAllister was more than a little interested in what she was going to divulge about her personal life. No! Why should she explain herself to this ignorant buccaneer of a man . . . this barbarian in sheep's clothing? She clammed her mouth shut.

'Carry on. I'm all ears.'

'I'm sure you are. But I don't see what my personal life has to do with you.' Hope glowed inside. She had won that point. But she had forgotten whom she was crossing swords with, and Craig McAllister was not about to let her have the last word.

'Naturally, your personal life has nothing to do with me. However, may I remind you that you are a guest in my hotel and I feel a certain responsibility for your wellbeing. If you insist on going out at night, simply take a torch with you and tell someone where you are going.'

'I object to having to report to you like a child.'

'Perhaps if you didn't behave like a child it wouldn't be necessary.'

She had fallen right into that one. She could sense his smug self satisfaction. She tugged ineffectually at her burning aching wrists. Her feet were cold, her wrists were hurting her, and suddenly she felt very downhearted. All she wanted to do was to go in and put some distance between herself and the odious Craig McAllister.

'Let me go!'

'Only if you promise not to assault me again.'

There was silence. Hope wasn't about to promise this brute anything. In the distance she could hear the gentle waves lapping on the sand. Her idyllic moonlit paddle seemed a million miles away—Craig McAllister took the enjoyment out of everything. Hope gritted her teeth in resistance.

'No. I don't know when you will provoke me again.'

'Then you will remain my prisoner.' He tightened his grip.

'Ow. You're hurting me. You bully.' He laughed at that, a cruel empty sound.

'No one's ever called me a bully before.'

'Your other victims were probably too frightened.'

'And you're not?'

'Of you? Of course not!' It was all a bluff. At this moment Hope felt the power and dominating will of this arrogant man. But she wasn't going to let him know that. She tugged again at her confined wrists. 'I want to go in,' she hissed angrily.

'And I want your promise that you won't slap me again.'

How she hated this man. No one had ever dared to treat her like this before.

'OK. You don't give me any choice do you? I promise.'

Craig released her hands and Hope started to rub them; they were burning from his touch and she had to try to erase the sensation of his strong warm hands from her memory.

'You're nothing more than a big bully Craig McAllister. Do you realise that? A hateful bully.'

'I still have your promise . . .'

'I didn't mean it.'

'You gave me your word.'

'Maybe I'm not the sort of person who keeps their word . . .'

'Oh . . . I think you are . . .' There was an intimate knowing sound to his voice now, and his eyes, now accustomed to the dull light, raked over her features making Hope feel as though she was pinned, exposed and totally known to him.

'Let's get inside, Miss Barraclough.' There was fatigue, but also gentle humour in his tone

67

now. 'I'm tired, hungry and getting cold. Come on,' he growled. He had started to walk towards the hotel.

'I can't yet. I've got to put my shoes on. '

'Oh woman! You're just trouble aren't you? Pick up your shoes.' Hope hesitated. 'Go on. Pick them up.' He walked back towards her. 'What on earth possessed you to go paddling in this weather?'

He moved closer and closer to her, stopping in front of her. He was so close Hope could hear his steady breathing and sense the power coiled within him. Then, wordlessly, he stretched out a strong muscular arm and wrapped it around Hope's shoulder whilst he slipped the other arm under her legs, lifting her up in his arms, cleaving her close to his tight, muscular body.

The shocking strangeness of it all took Hope's thoughts away. She felt his hot breath fanning her cheeks, her bones were as putty in his arms. She wound her free arm hesitantly round his shoulder and her fingers made contact with the silky soft hair at the nape of his neck. Startled at the strange heat that coursed through her she moved her hand so that it rested neutrally on his brushed cotton shirt. Even then Hope could feel the tight hard muscles of Craig's back, sense the bodily warmth beneath the clothes and imagine the virile male animal who held her in his arms.

At that moment the moon emerged from

behind the clouds and threw a pale silvery light on Craig's distinctive features. He no longer appeared the harsh unapproachable adversary. All that she could see was a strong highly attractive male who projected an air of quiet strength and overwhelming masculinity. Her heart was thumping in her breast as Craig turned and started to walk back to the hotel, carrying her in his powerful yet gentle arms.

All too soon it seemed he was scrunching across the gravel, arriving outside the lobby of the hotel. Hope didn't want this close confinement to end. She had become enmeshed in an irresistible pull of the senses, overwhelmed by a wave of sensuality such as she had never experienced in her life. She felt drunk, drugged in the excited strangeness of it all, drunkenly swooning, borne along on a tide of strong masculine power and unassailable male charisma.

She turned to him then, her pert face innocent and calm, her wide green eyes looking steadily at him, staring into his eyes but she was not prepared for what she found there. The sudden intensity of his gaze was stirring every cell in her body. She felt mesmerized as his dark assertive eyes feasted on her pale face, her bright emerald eyes sparkling out their own messages of attraction and sensual desire. He didn't say a word, but noiselessly he dropped his face closer and closer to hers, until Hope felt certain that he was going to kiss her, and she knew as she'd never known anything in her life that she would not, could not, repulse his kiss.

CHAPTER SIX

But then Hope had the strangest sensation. As Craig looked at her his eyes suddenly became dull and glazed—like one of those awful stuffed animals festooning the walls of the lobby. Now it seemed as though he were looking through her, not seeing her, his face becoming that cold empty mask she had seen so many times before. Silently he loosened his hold on her and she dropped softly, noiselessly, her bare feet landing on the thickly carpeted floor.

'There's a torch under the desk over there.' He nodded in the direction of reception. 'Use it the next time you feel like a moonlit walk. Clouds have a habit of getting in the way.'

She watched as he stalked away. She didn't know what was going on between her and Craig, she couldn't even begin to understand, but all she knew was that every time he walked away from her there was unfinished business left between them.

The following day she woke determined to make a start. She dressed in heavy grey cords and a lemon jumper and made her way down. She called out when she reached the dining-room. It was a little after eight. She wanted to eat and get on her way. No one responded to her call. Somehow it didn't surprise her: she

71

was growing used to the feeling that she had become invisible since she had set foot on the island.

She heard voices, a man's and a woman's, in the kitchen. She called out again, but still no one responded. She pushed through the swinging door into the kitchen and the voices stopped immediately. Craig and Mrs. McClennan looked at her, leaving her with the distinct impression that she might as well be an alien from another planet.

'Good-morning,' she said with false breeziness, a falsetto note in her voice. Silence descended on the kitchen like a shroud, sending squirming tension screaming through Hope's body. 'I did call out but no one seemed to hear me.'

Mrs. McClennan looked up. 'Why didn't you sit down at your table? I would have come out to you in a moment.'

The message was loud and clear, as if it had been shouted from the rooftops. She should not be in the kitchen, she was not welcome there. But now she was here she wasn't about to sound the retreat, a little voice inside her head forced her to stand her ground.

'I'll make a start today with the bird census. Is there some way I can get to Strainay Cove?'

Mrs. McClennan's face tautened, her mouth becoming a grim line. She stared first at Hope and then at Craig before getting up from the table and walking towards a huge steaming pot on the range. And Hope was left wondering what on earth she'd said that had caused such obvious offence.

Hope's stomach clenched. There was only so much silence, so much hostility she could take. She was beginning to tremble and when she spoke her voice had a tiny quaver in it. 'Then I suppose I'll have to walk . . . It can't be more than two miles.'

Craig drained his mug and stood up, walking towards her.

'I want a word with you.'

'Oh good. Are you going to fix up some transport for me?' she asked spikily. Perhaps it was nervousness that made her gabble and crack facetious comments whenever he was around. He had a face like thunder, she didn't know what his intention was but co-operation had nothing to do with it.

'I want a word with you. In private,' he added for emphasis, grabbing her by the elbow and turning her around.

'Hey!' she yelled. 'Take your hands off me.'

'Into my office now,' he spat out angrily and Hope found herself being propelled along the corridor into a large low-ceilinged room in which bookshelves covered every conceivable inch of wall space. Craig pressed her into a dark brown leather armchair, and as soon as he removed the pressure from her shoulders she sprang up again like a jack-in-the-box.

'What the hell do you think you're playing

at?' she yelled, trying to get to the door, but finding the exit blocked by his tall lean body.

'Sit down. We need to talk.'

'Oh do we? How convenient for you. I've needed to talk to you since I set foot on the island. I've asked about office space. No comment. I've asked about transport. No comment. But when it suits you, I'm frog-marched in here.'

'You're on my territory.'

'And you don't ever let me forget it, do you?' He was wearing down every ounce of resolution and strength she possessed and she slumped back exhaustedly into the armchair.

'You shouldn't go out censusing today.'

'Why ever not? I need to make a start . . . I've already lost one day.'

'You might not have noticed but today is Sunday.'

'Yes. I've noticed. I can tell you the date— even the year if you want.'

He wasn't impressed with her flippant remarks.

'I know on the mainland Sundays are basically like any other day of the week. Of course some people go to church, or they ritually eat a roast dinner, but basically they can shop and work as if it was any other day of the week. It's not like that on Branaigg. Everyone observes the Sabbath.'

'But surely no one would even notice if I sat in Strainay Cove counting birds.'

74

'You can't put a foot anywhere on this island without someone noticing. You're a stranger.'

'I don't need reminding,' she said peevishly. 'But there's so much to do. If I lose every Sunday I'll never get everything done.'

'It doesn't really matter, does it?'

'What do you mean?'

'This survey was all a cosmetic exercise. A delaying tactic. Sending you out here was a cheap way of buying time for the oil company.'

'That is ridiculous!'

'I've been dealing with the oil company for over a year now. Nothing is ridiculous.'

'I'm not their employee though. My survey is independent.'

'One person? With three weeks? What exactly do you think you can achieve?'

The thought had crossed her mind more than once. In her darkest hours she imagined coming away from the island having achieved nothing. If the weather was bad she would be able to achieve little. But there was a tiny voice in her head full of optimism and determination, and this voice told her she could achieve everything she set out to, if she put her mind and energies to it.

'I'll get a lot more done if everyone stops putting barriers in my way. You just want to hamper the survey. This Sunday business is very convenient for you.'

'Look.' He growled. He was leaning against his desk and he gripped the table with his fingers, tensing them until they were bone-white. 'I don't want you here but that's not the reason I'm trying to stop you working today. If I really wanted to mess things up for you I wouldn't have mentioned anything at all about the Sabbath. I could have let you go out unaware of the strength of feeling on the island and you would have destroyed, in one fell swoop, any good feeling there might be towards you.'

'I haven't come across much good feeling so far.'

'You have to give the islanders time. Not everyone is—'

'Like you? Then there's a chance for me yet,' she cut in spikily, her green eyes flashing fire.

'I'll take you out first thing tomorrow.'

'Isn't there a car I can hire somewhere?'

'This isn't London. Every car or van or tractor is in use. I'll see what I can do. I'll ask around today. But I'll take you to Strainay Cove tomorrow morning. First thing.'

'I'll believe it when I see it.'

'Big city cynicism?'

'No. I just have this feeling that things will keep going wrong.'

'And I thought your name was Hope?' His voice was unexpectedly soothing and Hope felt colour rushing into her cheeks. She lifted her chin defiantly.

'It is. I haven't given up. I'm not giving up.

76

I'll do this survey if it kills me.'

'Such devotion to work. Sir Gregory would be impressed.'

'Maybe it's about time I spoke to him. There are one or two things we need to sort out. Any objection if I make a phone call?'

'To Sir Gregory?' He threw back his dark head and laughed. It was a cruel sound and it jarred on her nerves.

'Yes. As a matter of fact.'

'Be my guest.' He indicated an old-fashioned black telephone complete with braided brown cable. 'You have a hot-line to the chairman of the oil company I suppose?'

'No,' she said evasively.

'Is he a personal friend?'

'I've never met the man.'

'What makes you think you'll ever get through to him—even if you do find out where he is—and I doubt that very much.'

'Put your money where your mouth is then. Take me on a trip around the island if I get through to him.' She offered a hand, and Craig, a wry smile breaking out on his face, seized her tiny hand in his and shook it firmly.

'It's a deal.'

*   *   *

'I still don't understand how you did it.'

'I have my ways.' She'd never won an easier bet. Marcus had let it slip he was entertaining

77

Sir Gregory that weekend. The rest had been simple.

'I'm not sure that you play everything by the rules . . . I have a feeling that you're a street-fighting girl.' He stopped talking as he concentrated on driving.

'I thought there was an A road that circled the island.'

'There is. This is it.' The road was a tortuous single track which twisted around lochsides and bog hollows defying all sense of direction. They mounted a hill and he stopped the car overlooking a long strand of white sand. 'This is Strainay Cove.'

'Great.' She reached for the door, but a hand on her arm restrained her.

'How about telling me how you managed to get through to the Chairman of the oil company. *He's* more elusive than the Scarlet Pimpernel.'

She felt his firm grip on her arm, her heart was beating wildly and colour was flooding into her neck and cheeks as she fixed him with a steady green-eyed gaze.

'That's my secret.' She didn't trust him, couldn't trust him. The way he felt about her survey he would distort anything she told him to his own advantage.

'Is he your father? Uncle? Cousin third time removed?'

'No. I told you before, I've never met the man.'

'Tell me,' he insisted, a blaze of irritation in his voice, and she looked away, afraid to meet his penetrating glance, feeling his grip tighten on her arm.

'You can cut off the blood-supply to my arm if you want and I still won't tell you.'

He relinquished his hold on her. His eyes burned with a black fire. 'Where did they dredge you up from anyway? You're crazy. I heard you telling Sir Gregory a complete pack of lies.'

'I don't know what you mean,' Hope denied, knowing it was less than the truth.

'All that about us disrupting the next AGM. No one's ever said anything about that.'

'It might have crossed your mind though. It's just the sort of publicity oil companys hate these days.'

'Whose side are you on?'

'I'm not on anybody's side. Can't you get that into your thick skull?' She could hear a slightly desperate tone to her voice and it frightened her.

'Yes I forgot. You're independent. Prepared to play one off against the other if it means getting what you want in the end. Just exactly what is it you're after? What's your price? What was that phone call all about?' She looked up at him, half-frightened at the pulse beating in his neck, wondering if he'd heard her talk of collecting mussels. 'You tell *me.* You seemed to have eavesdropped most of my

79

conversation.'

'I only overheard the part about AGMs and frustrated fishermen and farmers. You made it sound as though everyone was about to man the barricades.'

'And aren't you? Or is it all talk?'

He had this way of ignoring questions he didn't want to answer. He stared at her, his eyes travelling over her pale face as if trying to unravel the workings of her mind. 'I don't trust you. Tell me what that phone call was all about.'

'No. I don't trust you . . . Look . . .' She was angry now, it boiled up inside her and she met his dark intimidating stare unflinchingly. 'Leave me here and I'll walk back to the hotel when I'm ready. I am allowed to *walk* on a Sunday I presume?' She flung the car door open, glad to feel fresh air on her face, glad to be out of the fuggy overheated atmosphere that always developed whenever she was in Craig McAllister's company.

She took a deep cleansing breath, closing her eyes, concentrating on the scent that tantalized her nostrils. There was a distinct smell to the island: seaweed, rain and peat-smoke, it was both acid and enlivening. Above her were cliffs, rising like sentinels over the wind-tortured marran grass. Before her was the path through rocks and sand dunes to Strainay Cove. She started to walk towards the sea. The sounds of wind and sea were inseparable on that wild afternoon. She stopped, overlooking the bay. She licked her lips, her skin salt and Atlantic-kissed.

Suddenly she knew he was behind her, she sensed his presence, the hairs on the back of her neck prickling atavistically.

'I'm not leaving you here.' His voice was almost lost in the blustery wind. He walked to her side. He stood over her, dominating her. He had no right to intimidate her so. She screwed up her courage and spoke.

'And I'm not telling you how I phoned up Sir Gregory or what my conversation was about.'

His eyes contracted and his mouth became a grim line and Hope sensed that he was going to change the subject, he always did when things got hot.

'When you've finished admiring the scenery I'll take you on a bit further. We'll have to get a move on though. I haven't got all day.'

She turned towards him, her arms pulled into the baggy over-long sleeves of her jumper, feeling cold in the buffeting wind.

'Just let me find my own way home—I mean back to the hotel.' She squirmed at her slip, catching the reaction in Craig's eyes as they twinkled before dulling away to darkness again. The Castle Hotel could never be home.

But then he looked at her, his glance both penetrating and subtly tantalizing. 'No. I'm not leaving you.'

He said it in a soothing tone that went deep inside her, coiling around her, leaving her warm. It was several seconds before she realized that he had said that without any mockery, or cynicism or anything that would detract from the simple message of his words. She trembled, turning away from the breakers, the marron grass and the dark forbidding sea, noting the oil-blackened tips of the rocks on the waterline before she strode purposefully back to the car. She hesitated before opening the car door, watching as Craig opened his.

She knew she had to keep her wits about her. He was spinning a web around her, taking her senses away, dominating her and then treating her softly, gently, trying to confuse her.

'You make it seem as though you're trying to protect me, don't you? But this vigilance is just a convenient way of keeping me under close scrutiny. You want to know what I'm up to, don't you?'

He stared at her, his eyes contracting to dark slits as he appraised her tousled hair and her wind-blown cheeks. 'If you're up against someone who doesn't play by the rules you have to be prepared to play dirty too.'

CHAPTER SEVEN

She hadn't come to Branaigg to play complicated power games, but that was the way things seemed to be going. Even when Craig appeared to be co-operating with her she couldn't trust him. She'd sensed that his promise to take her to the Cove in the morning was a lie. She knew it in her bones even before she got out of bed and as she opened the curtains she could see that his car wasn't there. And now it was ten. She'd been kicking her heels around the hotel for two hours and frustration boiled up in her like a pressure-cooker on full heat.

She rehearsed over and over again the exact words she was going to lambast Craig McAllister with. *He* thought he could string her along with promises—promises which he had no intention of ever fulfilling. Was he punishing her for being secretive about that phone call? He seemed to think he had a God-given right to know everything that she was planning to do. She stalked up and down the lobby, flicking her wild gingery hair off her face, her pert features creased into a frown; too annoyed to sit down, or read or to do anything other than simmer with impotent rage.

And then she heard the tell-tale sound of

his car tyres crunching on the gravel and she spun out of the hotel door.

'Where the hell have you been? You told me we could leave at eight.'

He walked around the front of the car and Hope noticed that his dark brown cords were caked in mud. He looked as though he had been wallowing in the stuff, even the arms of his cream jumper were stained brown.

'I was called away,' he informed her perfunctorily, without a flicker of reaction on his face.

He knew she was furious, but he ignored her mood, taking her anger to an even higher gear.

'An errand of mercy I suppose?'

'Yes. It was as a matter of fact. How perceptive of you,' he added, angry sarcasm in his tone. Hope felt her heart clench and her mouth dry. She sensed something serious had happened that morning which made her foul-tempered attack on him totally inappropriate; now her humiliation would follow.

'I had a phone call at seven. It was from Mrs. McGregor. Her husband was out ploughing his land and the tractor went over on him. He was trapped underneath.'

'Oh God!' Hope wailed. She had known accidents like this at home, a cousin had been crippled by a tractor and her eyes filled up with tears. 'Is he alive? Is he OK?'

'What does it matter to you? All *you* care

84

about is your precious survey.'

'That's not fair. How is he?' She looked at Craig and he gave her a sullen closed look, tiredness etched about his eyes.

'Tell me!' she insisted.

'Just stick to your survey and forget about the islanders.'

'No!' He was about to walk past her and she tentatively put out a hand and pressed it against his chest. Her touch was the barest fingertip connection, but a strange heat burned through her body at the contact.

He stopped.

His mouth was a tight thin line and his gaze travelled from her outstretched hand to her eyes where he stared fiercely into her face as though he hated the very sight of her. A terrible shudder ran through Hope's body and she dropped her hand, letting it hang loosely at her side.

'His legs were both crushed. The doctor says it's going to be touch and go whether he loses them.'

'Oh,' she murmured, her face creasing with pain, her eyes wet with tears. 'Do they have a family?'

'Two young boys. No one who can run the farm for him. Life was hard enough as it was. He was ploughing on difficult hilly land—land he doesn't usually bother with, but his crops are poorer without the seaweed he used for manure and he needs every inch of land . . . of course last year's seaweed was destroyed by the oil.'

'I'm sorry.'

'Apologies come easily to you, don't they?'

'Why are you so nasty to me? The tanker disaster wasn't my fault. Every time I apologize to you you take my words and throw them back in my face.' Her voice faltered and she knew that any moment now she would burst into tears, her eyes glistening in sorrow and pain.

He stared at her, a timeless dark-eyed stare as though he had no emotions left in him, as though everything, anger, concern, pain, everything had been spent. She knew before he opened his mouth that he wouldn't respond to her impassioned outburst; he simply ignored her emotions as though they left him cold.

'I'll be ready in about half an hour. As you can see, I need a shower, a change of clothes and something to eat.'

'Shall I just take the car myself? Bring it back at lunch-time? You must be exhausted.'

He stared coldly at her as though she had just spoken totally out of turn.

'I'll be ready in about half an hour. Put your things in the car. The boot's open.'

They drove in silence to the Cove. He stopped the car at the top of the cliffs and started to get out.

'There's no need . . . I can get my things out

86

of the boot.'

He ignored her instruction without so much as a backward glance. He unloaded her coat, telescope and backpack.

'When do you want to pick me up again?' There was a quaver in her voice, it was awkward talking to him, a constant battle to keep any communication between them on an even keel.

'I'll be here at one.'

'One? I was hoping to stay out until dark. I've missed so much time already . . . there's such a lot to do . . .' The words were out of her mouth before she had a chance to think. He would imagine that she was trying to get at him. It wasn't true. She couldn't face any more scenes at the moment.

His face was unreadable. She waited nervously for his response, her stomach knotting, he confused and intimidated her, there was never any way of predicting his reaction to her, she knew so little about him.

'I could pick you up sometime after six,' he uttered in an unexpectedly quiet voice, his eyes resting on her calmly. 'Are you sure that's what you want?'

'Yes. That would be perfect.' Her green eyes glinted with delight, fading when they met his remote gaze.

'You see that cottage up there?' He swivelled around and pointed to a grey-white stone cottage nestling in the hillside a few hundred yards away.

'Yes.'

'That's the Dundonalds'. I've told them that you will be here. They will be expecting you to call on them whenever you want a break.'

'It's OK. I badgered Mrs. McClennan into making me some sandwiches. I've a flask of hot tea as well.'

A frown formed across his face before he spoke again, and when he did he uttered each word slowly and with deliberate emphasis as if talking to someone who had a poor grasp of the language.

'The Dundonalds will be expecting you. They will be very offended if you don't call.'

Sometimes it seemed that every time she opened her mouth she put her foot in it. When she wasn't crossing swords with Craig McAllister she was hurtling headlong into some sort of culture clash, in trying to be helpful she only succeeded in causing even more offence.

'You can't stay out here all day perched on a rock. You won't last a week, never mind three,' he added authoritatively.

'I'll be fine . . . I come from a hardy line.' She looked up at Craig and her mouth quivered. His concern confused her, she liked the feel of it, it sent a warm sensation through her body that seemed to protect her from the buffeting wind gusting at her back.

He helped her with her coat and handed her

the backpack. 'The islanders want to make you welcome. It's not fair to take everything out on you. Like you said, the oil disaster wasn't your fault . . . Please. Call in on the Dundonalds'.'

She nodded silently, swallowing hard. He had spoken without a trace of cynicism, anger or aggression. Simple, honest words and that knowledge coiled around her bringing a flush to her face.

'Well 'bye then,' she managed.

He seemed to hesitate and she caught his mood, fidgeting slightly with her backpack instead of moving off down the cliffs.

'Before you go.' He touched her arm gently and she stopped still, her body shocked, darting quivers of heat rushing along her arm where he had touched her. 'I owe you an apology . . . I shouldn't have spoken to you the way I did back at the hotel . . . the accident . . . I said some very cruel things . . . I . . .'

His dark eyes met hers and suddenly Hope felt as though she were melting from the inside out, her stomach fluttering and her heart starting to race. He had touched a chord deep inside her, unknown emotions called out for release. She stared, her eyes fixed on his dark face, noting the concern in his face, trying to find her voice. The play of emotion on his face held her mesmerized. A glow of warmth dispersed the shadows in his eyes and softened his features.

'Please . . . I understand.' She heard her

89

own voice, soothing and gentle, it sounded strange and new to her as though another person had spoken the tender words. At that moment she felt an overwhelming desire to wrap her arms around the big man and kiss him, love him to unconsciousness. The thought lasted a brief moment until she checked herself, hurtling the crazy notion out to space. 'Let's forget about it,' she added, trying to force an impersonal professional tone into her voice.

'Here. Take this.' He handed her a green waterproof coat. She had one like it back at home, in Wales. This one looked much bigger. 'You'll probably have to roll the sleeves up but it'll keep the rain off if you get caught in a shower.'

'It looks like it's going to be a fine day.' Hope looked up at the clear blue sky. 'Not a cloud to be seen.'

'The weather on Branaigg changes in the twinkling of an eye.' He paused, staring at her. 'You'll have to learn not to judge everything by appearances.'

He was looking at her in a way that made her nerve-ends curl in the most peculiar manner. She grabbed the coat, feeling heat rushing into her face, not understanding why her emotions always seemed to go haywire whenever he was around.

'I'll see you later then,' she said in a voice that had a falsely breezy note to it. She looked at him briefly, noting his eyebrow raised in quiet reaction and then she turned and set out towards the dunes, relieved to be out of the company of this deeply disturbing male.

She slipped down the sandy path on to the wide beach; the telescope in its leather case slung over her shoulder like a gun, the backpack containing her recording equipment, binoculars, flask and food, bouncing against her spine as she walked.

In the past, bird censuses had shown that the rocky headland was a favourite breeding ground for some of the more unusual birds and Hope wondered whether they had returned this year. She managed to find a sheltered nook in amongst the rocks above the shoreline and here she settled in with her binoculars, telescope and note-pad.

Time sped by; she was captivated by the beach, the solitude, the simplicity of it all. In no time at all she started to spot species, birds on the headland, nesting at the top of tiny fingers of rock that stretched out to sea. Sanderlings, ringed plovers and turnstones foraged in some half-buried kelp whilst a party of red-shanks bickered, chasing, flying round a sand pool.

Her head was clear, her mind and body energized, in harmony with nature. When she looked up she saw a clear blue sky dotted with tiny powder-puff clouds. The sun was at her back, warming, soothing, and in her sheltered nook the wild westerly wind drove over her head leaving her with the feeling of being snugly tucked in against the driving island elements.

'Do you ever come up for air?'

Hope looked up, startled by the voice. A woman stood at the top of the gully. She was tall and broad, middle-aged, grey showing in the wind-tousled black of her hair. Her feet were clad in heavy wellington boots, her legs in bottle-green woollen trousers, the same shade picked out in her flecked jumper.

'I'm Mrs. Dundonald. I've been expecting you. I saw Craig drop you off hours ago. I thought maybe you were too shy to call.'

Hope looked at her watch. It was almost one. 'I didn't realise the time.' That morning she had been able to study as attractive a gathering of waders as any birdwatcher could wish for. She had made copious notes, and, for a while, she didn't know how long, she had been captivated by curlews standing about on fingers of rocks fifty yards away, her mind fixed in total concentration.

'I've a fresh-brewed pot of tea, some fresh-baked bread and scones.' The woman studied Hope for a few seconds as she stood up, her eyes crinkled in the bright sunshine to heavy lidded sea-blue triangles. 'Looks to me as though you could do with fattening up a bit.'

'I've heard that somewhere before. Mrs. McClennan seems to think I need a few extra pounds.'

'More than a few,' came the cryptic reply.

As they approached the cottage, stepping across the spongy grass, the smell of fresh baking came out to greet Hope and when she crossed the threshold, her eyes taking some time to adjust to the dull light, her senses were besieged by nostalgic thoughts of home, the heady yeasty atmosphere taking her back to her childhood.

They had walked right into the kitchen, a large room dominated by a vast peat burning stove set into a broad stone fireplace. It was made of heavy black iron, all shiny from polishing, pipes of the same weighty cast-iron running from the stove into the wall behind, taking hot water around the cottage. Mrs. Dundonald opened the doors of the stove and red heat from the burning peat forged forward. There was no flame, only this pulsing red of the peat and she spread her hands in front of the heated glow, rubbing them together.

'Come and sit by the warmth a minute whilst I set the table.' She motioned to a faded chintz-covered armchair which, with its partner, nestled close to the stove.

Mrs. Dundonald liked to talk. She told Hope, as she tucked into the homely fare, that she had three grown-up sons, all working or studying on the mainland. Her husband farmed the land, and she was related one way or another to everyone on the island. Hope relaxed, filling up with food, relieved to find herself in the company of someone who didn't appear to have taken an instant dislike to her. Hope steered clear of any conversation about the survey, she wanted to enjoy this respite, afraid that this calm interlude might be shattered by a few wrongly chosen words . . . was life on Branaigg making her paranoid? She wondered.

The lunch was rounded off with sweet scones, warm, spread with butter that melted into the soft crumbly texture. Hope sipped the strong sweet black tea; she hadn't expected to like tea this way, had been surprised how fresh it seemed on her palate. She looked around the table at the cheese, fresh baked bread, the home-made pickles, and at that moment, more than any other she felt homesick, remembering her grandparents' farm, their own bleached white ancient kitchen table, in her memory always spread with home-made food in a similar fashion.

'The sea air gives you an appetite, doesn't it?'

Hope nodded, a lump in her throat.

'Make sure you come back tomorrow. I'll tell you some more about the island.'

Mrs. Dundonald had done most of the talking. And moreover she showed little interest in Hope's work. It suited Hope fine.

'Thanks again for the lunch Mrs.

Dundonald.'

'The lunch was nothing, Hope. And the name is Bella. Make sure you call again. We don't see many fresh faces around these parts.'

That afternoon there were a couple of light showers, nothing too disturbing, although the rain blew sand into her face, stinging sharp against her sunburnt cheeks.

Craig arrived promptly at six. She smiled a wary half-smile and he responded in kind, loading her things into the car, noting but not commenting on the drops of rain that spattered the coat he had lent her. Hope wondered if at last some sort of calm was coming into their relationship and she felt relieved; perhaps they might even be able to talk about her work, share insights.

It was a little after six as they passed through the harbour and out up the hill towards the Castle Hotel. They were both silent, Hope secretly waiting for that first glimpse of Traisay Bay, her bay, as the car mounted the hill. Reaching the crest of the hill, Craig stopped the car and got out. Hope followed, bemused.

He stood, the wind blowing his shiny brown hair off his face, an impressive man, tall and dominating, indomitable against the buffeting wind.

'Look at that. It's so beautiful.' He turned to her then, his eyes contracting as though she was a foreign body he needed to protect

95

himself from. Feeling stunned by the murderous glint in his ice cold eyes Hope realized that any feeling of harmony she had imagined between them was over.

'Of course . . .' Even the tone of his voice had altered. How she hated his voice when it was cold and harsh, it jarred every nerve in her body, she wanted to hear him speak in those warm caressing tones. 'Of course, I don't expect you to recognize beauty. Scientists aren't trained in aesthetic appreciation, are they? You simply count everything, analyse everything, take all the emotions, the beauty out of everything until it is stripped bare.'

Numbly Hope followed him back to the car.

He put his foot down on the throttle, the car sped down the hill. Hope sat there dazed, her throat constricted into a tight knot, for once totally lost for words. He was wrong, so wrong and there was no way, there would never be any way she could make him see the person she truly was.

CHAPTER EIGHT

It seemed as though an inevitable cold war had descended on their relationship; they grated on each other. Hope found the hairs on the back of her neck prickled whenever she sensed, with that strange sixth sense, that Craig was near. Their conversations became frigid, perfunctory statements that always left Hope feeling tense and uncomfortable. It was a draining experience.

Sometimes, in her room late at night she rehearsed little speeches she would make to Craig, listing her qualities and attitudes, making him see that she was not the cold-hearted scientist he took her to be. But, in the harsh light of day, he always seemed moody and unapproachable so her courage failed her and she was left to comfort herself with the thought that he would probably have laughed contemptuously at her placatory speech, delighted that his frigid style had forced her to grovel for acceptance.

And then, at other times, when she watched his haughty arrogant gait, studied his remote dark-bearded face, she wondered why she bothered to think about him at all. She had come across difficult men before, hadn't she? He was a temporary cog in her wheel. Still, despite him she had managed to forge a working pattern, and, in a few weeks she would leave the island, and resume her London life. Inexplicably, thoughts of London always made her heart sink even more and she tried to hush the contradictory voices running around in her head.

At the hotel she still ate alone, working in her room until late each night, spreading maps and census records over every conceivable space, but she always knew when he was close by, some primitive warning system alerted her body, sending signals that demanded atavistic response.

Work was a comfort to her. Each day as she left the car, she put thoughts of Craig McAllister completely out of her mind. Out in the open, alone with her work, Hope found she slipped into an easy routine. The weather was kind to her that first week and the census moved along at a heady rate. She watched birds from morning 'til night, her eyes strained with the effort, and, eventually, out of all the noise and activity, themes and patterns began to emerge. She progressed so quickly at Strainay Cove that she was soon able to move on each afternoon—after lunch with the Dundonalds—to the neighbouring bay, Grannad.

Whereas Strainay was a wide sandy beach, fringed with dunes, dotted with marron grass that tossed about in the wind, its headlands carved from the angular black rocks, Grannad

98

presented a far harsher profile.

The cove was steep-sided, carved from the black rock cliffs and the lower shoreline was not a gentle sandy inlet, but a hazardous array of rocky outcrops running in sharp-topped ridges to the sea, dividing the cove into a series of tiny sandpools and rocky inlets.

If Strainay Cove was nature with a gentle face on it, Grannad, with its harsh sounding name, was nature in the raw. Seaweed, some of it black and despoiled, lay in heaps along the beach, torn up and evicted from the sea by gales. Huge waves plunged down on to the rocks, crashing thunderously, foam and spray spewing out, thrusting forth in a rhythmic intensity. Every time Hope stood at the top of the cliffs, hesitating before she plunged down towards the forbidding cove, she wondered at the awesome strength of the sea.

Grannad's rocky headland was a favoured breeding ground for a variety of seabirds, whilst, on a tiny island just off the coast, hundreds of blackheaded gulls squabbled for an inch of space: through her telescope Hope found that the island was solid with gulls sitting tail to tail, beak to beak. From time to time the squawking of the birds drifted in on the wind, a cacophony of noise which competed with the calls of gannets, guillemots and fulmars high up on the headland.

By Friday afternoon, Hope had marked scores of maps with little symbols representing birds. She had covered the same ground over and over again, mapping and recording, and she was beginning to recognize individual birds and breeding pairs. Her first week had been a series of days of sunshine and showers, walking and sitting, watching and recording and now as she tramped back towards Strainay Cove she felt pleased with herself.

Approaching the cove, she spotted Craig's car. She checked her watch. It was only a quarter to six. He was early. Normally she was back at the cove before he arrived. She hadn't told him about her visits to Grannad, for some reason she felt a need to keep her movements secret and until now she had successfully covered her tracks by returning before he arrived.

Suddenly his dark head appeared out of the sand dunes and he started to walk towards her. Hope felt the blood rush to her sunburnt face. He stopped in front of her, blocking her passage.

'Had a good afternoon?'

'Yes. Thank you.'

'Your first visit to Grannad?'

Hope looked up into his face, something she didn't understand was in his eyes, and it made her even more uneasy.

'No . . . I've been there before . . .' she said evasively.

'Why didn't you tell me?'

'I didn't realize I had to get your permission

100

to move about the island.'

'Don't you know the cove is hazardous? Rip-tides? Sinking sand?'

She found herself blushing, stammering for words. His words were harsh, but something in his face spoke of concern and her body prickled with strange emotions. 'I wasn't planning on taking a dip.' She managed a fake smile which died on her lips before it ever reached her eyes. Flippancy seemed her only defence against the heady emotional waters he always took her to.

'Someone must be *really* making it worth your while for you to go to so much trouble.'

It was such a cynical remark it wasn't worthy of a response and she just threw him a dirty look. He caught the look in her eyes and stared at her and there was something she didn't understand in his look as it floated over her.

'Don't you care about your own safety at all?'

'I've been fine . . . I'm very cautious,' she stammered. 'Mrs. Dundonald told me about the tides, and pointed out the best way down.'

He stared at her, that remote-eyed stare she was growing used to, and then he threw out an arm towards her. Hope flinched involuntarily, her limbs going weak with unadulterated fear. His eyes widened on her face for a moment and then he slipped the telescope from her shoulder along with the backpack and, without a word headed back to the car.

They were almost in Castlebay before he broke the silence.

'Why didn't you tell me you were going to Grannad? You've been going there all week, haven't you?'

'I . . .' Hope stumbled, trying to formulate some words in her mind and failing.

'I suppose I'm just the taxi driver.'

She hadn't ever thought of him in that light, he was a man of such pride and dominating presence, but now she could see her secrecy had hurt him, injured his self-esteem. For one all too brief moment it gave her a fierce surge of pleasure to know that she had broken through his arrogant self-possession. But then, inexplicably she suddenly felt an overwhelming desire to reach out and touch him, to stroke away his pain. It only lasted a moment. Shocked, frightened at the awesome strength of her unknown emotions, as though she were being engulfed by a tidal wave of primal feelings coming from the very heart of her, she slammed down a shutter tight, becoming once again the cool-headed scientist.

'If you found me a car you wouldn't need to take me everywhere.'

'I told you, there isn't one.'

'Did you try McGregor's garage? Mrs. Dundonald says he often hires out a car in the summer.'

He slammed on the brakes, the car

shuddered to a halt on the harbour front. Hope was thrown forward and then back against the seat with a dull thud, feeling the wind knocked out of her.

He turned on her then, like a raging bull, his eyes dark and dangerous. 'Don't you trust me at all? Don't you believe I tried to find you a car?'

She sensed his hurt and was unprepared for it.

'I . . .' she stammered, feeling the blood rushing up her neck and into her face, watching that fevered pulse pounding in Craig's neck.

'You have to go behind my back . . . you—'

'It wasn't like that.'

'No?'

'No.'

'I did make enquiries. Shall we check with Alex? See if he's prepared to back up my story? Though of course you wouldn't believe him anyway—we islanders are all in this together, aren't we? For your information Alex McGregor has a Metro he hires out. Unfortunately it is off the road at the moment. He is waiting for parts. Satisfied?'

He frightened her. The intensity of his emotions was beyond anything she had known in her life. He hated her. She sensed it. There was nothing about her that he admired or liked. Her heart hammered out its relentless tattoo, her throat tightened, tears welling up in her eyes. She had to get out of the car, out of the claustrophobic atmosphere. She reached out a hand and grabbed the door-handle, shocked to see that her hand was shaking.

'Where are you going?'

She didn't answer, she couldn't answer, her trembling voice would have given her away.

The wind whipped the tears from her face, she wiped the wetness from her cheeks and took a few deep breaths. The hairs on the back of her neck prickled, she sensed that he was behind her.

'Are you coming?'

'No.'

Somehow he sensed her hurt and when he spoke again his voice was calmer, the anger gone.

'Come on, Hope.'

The unexpectedly soft intonation of her name sent a curious shiver down her spine. She turned then, her green eyes still glistening wet.

'I've got to drop some mussels off for tomorrow's ferry.'

'Drop them off and we'll get back,' he coaxed soothingly.

'No. I'll walk back.' Nothing on this earth would make her get back in that car with him.

'Don't you think you've done enough walking for one day?' He was right of course. Her legs, her arms, even her eyes were aching and she had been looking forward to a relaxing hot bath.

'Don't you think I'm fit?' she countered, feeling cornered.

'Why do you have to answer my question with another question?'

Her lower lip quivered in reaction, her eyes brightened, flashing out strident green light. 'Because . . . because . . . because you seem to think you have the right to monitor my every movement . . . because being in your company is like being . . . suffocated.'

He threw back his head and laughed. Not the cruel cynical sound that she had witnessed before, but a rich deep warm sound that seemed to come from the heart of the man. 'You must hate me.'

'Yes. Yes I do,' she answered sulkily, regretting the words as soon as they left her mouth, frightened at the reaction she might provoke. But when she looked into his face she saw his eyes were bright with laughter and she relaxed.

He turned and opened the boot. 'Let's find these mussels.'

Hope delved into the backpack and produced a plastic container.

'Here.' She held it up for inspection.

He touched her outstretched hand, turning it at an angle. 'What have you done to your hand?'

There was a long scratch across her hand, edged in dried blood. He clasped her hand in his and gingerly stroked it. She suddenly felt oddly breathless. A feeling of pleasure tingled through her veins and her heart pumped with extraordinary vigour.

'I had a close encounter with a fulmar,' she somehow got out in a choked voice.

'Does it hurt?'

'No. Not now.' It had hurt at the time, her pride as much as her skin. It was a long time since she'd overestimated the good nature of nesting fulmars. She always assumed her intuition, her natural caution would guide her, but today it had let her down. Perhaps it would let her down again.

'Do you need a tetanus?'

'No. I'm up to date on my injections.'

'Let Mrs. McClennan give you something to bathe it with when we get home,' he said gently, all the while his hand touching hers, making her skin tingle, sending a surge of heat coursing through her body. *When we get home.* The words ran insistently, round and round her head. She was locked in the black glitter of his eyes, falling, falling out of control. She had to put on the brakes before it was too late.

'I don't like fulmars,' she said brightly, looking out across the harbour, taking in a broad sweep of the boats and the bustling activity. 'Curlews and sanderlings are much more civilized. Fulmars always scratch and bite if they think you're too close.'

He dropped his hand away from hers, as if

sensing her withdrawal. 'They're only trying to protect their territory.'

'And what's your excuse?' she said sharply.

'For what?'

'Your scratchy behaviour to outsiders.'

A derisive smile twisted his lips. 'Maybe I'm just trying to protect my own territory.'

'There is such a thing as *over*-protection.' She raised an eyebrow and looked him full in the face. His eyes glittered with amusement and Hope felt confused, unsure what was coming next.

'We don't get on very well, do we?' His mouth broadened to a wide grin revealing a perfect set of white teeth. She caught his mood, suddenly felt light and carefrce, and started to chuckle, a warm bubble of laughter coming from her unexpected and rich.

'No. We don't get on very well,' she affirmed, smiling, bright light radiating out from her sunburnt face.

His appraising gaze ran over her and she had the feeling that he was looking at her and reassessing her, his eyes quick and observant, studying her every move.

'You should smile more often Hope. It suits you.'

Later, as they drove back to the hotel, Hope went over events in her mind, trying to understand how Craig had managed to coax her into travelling back with him when she had made up her mind to walk, wondering how he had managed to bring them close together when she had determined to keep him at a distance. He had worked some island magic on her and she would need to keep her wits about her. Already she had fallen head over heels in love with the island; she couldn't afford to fall in love with the man.

CHAPTER NINE

Hope spent Sunday cooped up in the hotel. Rain lashed down outside her room and huge rolling waves thundered down on Traisay's shore as she neatened up her census charts and copious notes. It was a relief, the following day, to leave the confines of her room and she threw herself wholeheartedly into her work at Strainay and Grannad.

Exhaustion seeped through every muscle as she slunk into her bath that night. She lingered in the bath, the skin on her fingers wrinkling, until the water became too cool for comfort. She wrapped a blue towelling robe around her and lounged on her bed, census charts scattered all around her.

She started to study one of the charts, but her eyes were tired, like the rest of her, and soon her eyelids drooped, her hand flopping lifelessly over the side of the bed, and the heavily spotted piece of paper, looking for all the world like a child's dot-to-dot puzzle, drifted glider-like to the floor, landing noiselessly amongst the hillocks of her socks and shirt.

She drifted into a half-dream state, vaguely aware that she was lying on her bed, but heavy with sleep and strange images, as though drugged by the heady pace of life itself. Images of Roger, and then Craig, swept before her eyes like people on a merry-go-round at a fair, rushing past as if in a blast of hot oily air, only to reappear and vanish all over again.

Roger and Craig, rocks and the sea, the pounding turbulent sea, and ever and again the images came and vanished until it was only Craig's image that appeared before her eyes, Craig, appearing as though he had taken on something of the turbulent rhythmic intensity of the sea, his dominating presence eliminating Roger, rubbing him out from the scene.

A heavy pounding burst on Hope's ears, and then silence, and again, in rhythm with her dream, the pounding resumed. Suddenly she realized that the pounding was not in her dream, but on her bedroom door. She lifted her head half-heartedly, feeling sluggish, as if pleasantly drugged, looking up to see Craig standing nonchalantly in the doorway, his arm resting against the frame. He stood there, his dark face shadowed, his long lean body casually graceful, a finger tapping rhythmically against the wall.

Confusion ranged in her head, dream-like images competed with the presence of the man, she struggled back to full consciousness.

'Now there's a pretty sight,' he joked, taking in a full view of her, her wild gingery locks spilling almost endlessly across the pillow, her shapely legs bare and pale, and her breasts

110

tightly outlined through the bubbly blue material of the robe.

Her heart started to thunder, the blood pulsing in her ears, and she shot upright, feeling his eyes fixed on her barely covered body. She tightened the robe around her, unwittingly heightening Craig's awareness of her feminine curves and interesting angles. Their eyes met for a second before Hope looked away, afraid at the intensity of his gaze, not understanding all that she had seen in his eyes, aware that his look still burned on her, colour rushing up her neck and into her sunburnt cheeks.

'What . . . what do you want,' she stammered, half enjoying his invasion of her room, half frightened at the strange emotions coursing through her sleep-drugged body.

'It's nearly eight. Mrs. McClennan sent me up to check on you. Your dinner's spoiling, Miss.'

Hope glanced automatically at her wrist, realizing too late that her watch was on the bedside table.

'Don't worry. We *can* tell the time here . . . when the little hand's on the eight and—'

'Spare me the droll humour. If you'd let me dress I'll be down in a minute . . . I must have fallen asleep.'

'Must have,' he affirmed ruefully, his dark eyes twinkling. 'You could go down like that . . . very fetching.'

Discs of colour ran into her cheeks and he noticed them, smiling, his eyes contracting to dark shiny slits. Silence fell over the room, heavy and cloying, making the breath catch in her throat and then he was looking at her and something inexplicable passed between them and was gone.

He looked around the room at the papers scattered about, on the bed, the floor, the dressing table, every conceivable space had been submerged in paper, like confetti in a churchyard.

'Knock on my office door when you've finished your meal. I think you need some more room, don't you?' His face had an unfamiliar candour about it. She could have reminded him that she'd asked for extra space days ago, but for some reason the words dried in her mouth.

She dressed carefully that night. She put on a pretty white blouse, edged around the neck and cuffs with delicate broderie anglaise. Her wardrobe was pretty limited, but she teamed the blouse with her swirling black velour skirt.

Mrs. McClennan was waiting for her when she reached the dining-room, her hands on hips.

'I wondered what had happened to you, girlie. You're working too hard you know.' She gave Hope a concerned look. 'And do you eat those sandwiches I make for you?'

Hope nodded.

112

Mrs. McClennan shook her head in mock despair. 'You're not getting any plumper are you?'

'I think it's in the genes. My father is very slim. My mother doesn't understand it either.'

'Well I've made you a nice pie. You like my pastry don't you?'

Hope nodded and her heart soared. It seemed as though Mrs. McClennan had dropped her defences towards her, she even managed a cautious half-smile before she trudged back towards the kitchen.

After eating Mrs. McClennan's glorious steak pie, the pastry golden-glazed and shiny, the meat succulent in a rich dark gravy, Hope knocked on Craig's door. She felt half-fearful, half-excited as she waited for the door to open, her hand still clenched in a furled fist.

All through dinner her mind had turned to him. His studying gaze, his words, but mainly the feeling of being in the presence of a vital heady male who had stepped out of her dream, a man whose sexuality, she now realized, was poised on a hair-trigger control, someone who only needed the slightest encouragement to give in to the desire and longing she had felt in his eyes.

'Ah,' he said, a dark twinkling in his eyes. He grasped her hand and pulled her across the corridor into a room Hope had never entered before. The vast high-ceilinged room was dominated by a huge snooker table. He

113

caressed the green baize with a slim long-fingered hand.

'Do you play?'

'No.'

'Neither do I. Shame eh? I thought you could spread all your maps out on it though, what do you think?'

Hope nodded, too bemused by his light-heartedness to speak; she'd never seen this side of his character before, and she reacted carefully, as though walking on eggshells.

'And . . . come with me,' he held up an index finger and beckoned her out of the room, past his office into another room.

'Welcome to the junk room.' The room was piled high with odd pieces of furniture; chairs, tables, lamp standards. 'Here,' he said, taking one end of a dark mahogany desk, 'help me with this.' Hope grabbed the other end of the desk, and stood, not moving, shrugging her shoulders, unsure of what to do next.

'We'll take it to the games room. For you.' He smiled lightly, almost breathless with excitement, and Hope wondered whether this could be the same man who had shouted at her a few days ago, the man who had resented her presence on the island, in short the man who had made her life a misery since she had set foot on Branaigg. Perhaps this was one of his tricks; was he trying the softly softly approach, to confuse her, before he was aggressive and antagonistic to her again?

114

'Come on,' he cajoled, a wry smile on his lips, his face free of dark motives. 'Wake up sleepyhead,' he crooned in a soft lingering tone.

When the desk was firmly planted in the room, at one side of a huge marble fireplace, Craig disappeared, reappearing breezily, armed with an office chair and a white anglepoise lamp.

'Can you use a computer?' he asked, plugging in the lamp.

'Yes. Sort of.'

'Would one be useful?'

'Yes. I suppose so.'

'I'm beginning to feel like Santa Claus.'

He smiled ruefully and left the room, reappearing a few minutes later with various pieces of computer equipment which he set up on the desk. 'It's quite compact. It still leaves a lot of desk room,' he informed her, as though it was suddenly important that she approved of what he was doing.

'I haven't used one of these before, though,' Hope murmured, hesitantly. She had this fear of computers she was only beginning to come to grips with. And like someone frightened of any dog other than the family pet, she wondered whether she could be happy with this unknown variety of computer.

'Don't worry. They're all pretty much the same. Sit down.' He tapped the back of the chair.

Feeling a bit like Daniel entering the lion's den, Hope tremulously took up her place, noting his raised brow, the quirky silent amusement on his darkly bearded face.

'Don't worry. The computer isn't like me.'

She looked at him, puzzled.

'It doesn't bite.

'Relax,' he crooned softly, his breath disturbing the tendrils of hair about her ear. He rested his hands on her shoulders, spreading out his fingers, sending burning heat radiating through her body, as though he had touched her with burning coals. She could feel the life, his life forging through his fingers.

He leant over and inserted a disc in the computer. He had a certain definable scent about him, clean, soapy and masculine. He told her what to do next and Hope tried to follow his instructions, all the time aware of the gentle pressure on her shoulders.

It shocked her, the electric contact of his touch, the sense of being captured by him, the impact of his sudden closeness, and then she felt overwhelmed by a powerful need to wipe away the feeling his touch had branded on her shoulder. She tried to concentrate on the computer, forcing his image out of her mind and somehow she managed to carry out his instruction.

'Well done!' he said softly, with a voice to match the touch of his slim fingers.

She always felt pleased with herself when

she accomplished something on a computer, and she turned to him, her face full of excitement, her green eyes brimming with the feel of success, like a child's.

'What do I do now?' she asked.

Their faces were inches apart, so close she could feel his breath on her cheek. His eyes darkened and she could feel his stare going to the very heart of her, touching her somewhere deep inside, somewhere dark and unknown to her. The sudden intensity of his gaze sent colour forging up her neck and into her cheeks. Her pulse leapt out of control and began to thud visibly in the hollow at the base of her neck. She felt an unknown need coiling within her, alerting all her senses, trapping her in a dramatic mesh of male charisma. His lips were close, so close. One movement and all would be lost, she would tumble, tumble out of control. A tiny shiver shook her as his face came vividly alive, his dark eyes flickering with a glitter of intent, like a hunter marking out its prey. He hesitated. She could hear his heart thundering in wild hammer blows. His chest heaved in a harsh intake of breath. His eyes misted over and an expression of uncertainty flickered briefly across his features and was gone, replaced by a cold remote mask which sent a shudder down Hope's spine.

He pulled away from her, standing up straight, taking his hands from her shoulders.

'I'll find a couple of discs for you to store

117

your information on. You won't need my help any more.'

It seemed very important to him that she knew this. His voice was clipped and unaccountably rough and as he withdrew from the room Hope noticed that his body had lost some of its fluidity, his movements were tense and jerky and her stomach clenched as she tried to understand what was going on between them.

CHAPTER TEN

'I've just received a garbled message from the university.'

'Yes?' Hope swivelled round on her chair in the games room.

Craig was standing in the doorway, looking at her in a strange way that made her skin tingle, his eyes seeming to float over her body. Since the night when he had given her the computer she had seen very little of him. He had restored their relationship to a very formal basis. He avoided her in the hotel and their conversations were marked by a cold civility on his part, an awkward restraint which made Hope want to scream out in frustration.

'It was someone called Jake,' he said stiffly. 'He was in a hurry but he said "tell Hope the mussels are clean".'

'Oh,' she tried to keep the disappointment out of her voice.

'What's all the mystery?'

'Nothing,' she said evasively.

'What did all that mean?' he insisted.

'I was trying to find out what sort of shape the mussels are in.'

'Why?'

She felt torn between the need to let him know that she was looking into the fishermen's problems, and the need to be secretive. She

119

couldn't know if she could trust him. He looked at her, his dark eyes insistent, seeming to reach out to the heart of her.

'It was just a long shot . . . I wanted to see whether the mussels had been affected by the oil pollution. Mussels are a brilliant indicator of pollution . . . they filter fifty litres of water through their tissues every day. So, I collected mussels from the headland at Strainay . . .'

'But the mussels were clean.'

Hope nodded her head, her mouth a tight line.

'I still don't understand why you are looking at the sea-water. What's that got to do with the birds?'

She hesitated then, unsure of whether to let him know her aim. 'Not much,' she equivocated. Then she looked up at him and seeing his dark eyes on her she took a deep breath. 'But I'm looking at fishing as well now.'

'Since when?'

'Since the day I phoned Sir Gregory.'

'Why didn't you tell me?' There was barely concealed anger in his voice and Hope cringed, it would have been better to have kept her mouth shut. 'Why didn't you tell me when I asked you?'

She remembered that day, remembered how Craig had tried to make her tell him. She had resisted. She hadn't known him then. She hardly knew him now, he tried to keep himself remote from her, but sometimes the mask slipped and at those times she felt she knew everything about him.

She hesitated. 'I wanted some encouraging results first . . . and anyway,' she added spikily, 'I haven't seen much of you lately.'

She never knew where he disappeared to in the evenings. Sometimes she heard his car drive off as she changed after her day's work, other times, having spent the evening working in the games room, she heard his car return as she lay in bed, drowsy with sleep, the sound of his feet crunching over the gravel reassuring her in some strange way.

His eyes met hers and an unspoken message flashed between the two of them, quickly extinguished on both sides. Hope tensed, her stomach knotting, not understanding what she had seen, feeling out of her depth, aware he had alerted all her nerve-endings in a deeply disturbing way.

And then a cold mask fell over his face, his dark eyes moving over her features with a clear gleam of disappointment. When he spoke bitterness crept into his tone.

'So I suppose you think the fishermen are making a fuss about nothing?' he snapped caustically, his dark eyes laced with contempt. Hope's stomach clenched in fear and then she took a deep cleansing breath. Suddenly it was important to have it all out with Craig.

'You don't like me much, do you?'

'What gives you that impression?'

'I'm not blind.' She felt inexplicably angry, suddenly goaded to temper by the confusion he caused in her. He was hot and cold, gentle and aggressive; it was driving her demented.

He tensed, biting his bottom lip before he spoke again. 'It's nothing personal.'

'Isn't it?' she countered, confused to see colour forging into his high cheek-bones.

'My argument's with the oil company. You and I are looking at the same problem from different angles—like looking down a telescope from opposite ends—we have different priorities, different perspectives.'

'I don't see it like that at all. *You* need the facts. *I* need the facts,' she said, hating his antagonistic tone, trying to protect herself behind her cool scientific mask.

'It's all facts and figures to you, isn't it?' He had picked up the aloofness in her tone, his antennae tuned in to her nuances, and it enraged him even more. 'One oil disaster is pretty much the same as another to you, isn't it? You're so cold and analytical.'

Colour rushed into her cheeks. 'And I suppose you're all heart?' she retorted sarcastically, trying to protect herself against his attack, hating the way he confused her scientific façade with the person underneath, wishing there was some way she could convince him that she wasn't the person he seemed to think she was.

'Only a person with a stunted emotional

growth would mock feelings,' he said smugly.

That last remark was one too many. Hope stood up, her hands on her hips, looking up at the powerful man who stood before her.

'And I suppose you've cornered the market on feelings have you? Feelings won't get the islanders compensation. Solid hard facts are the only way. These,' she said expansively, stretching out her arm and making a broad sweep of the room which she had covered in maps, files, reports and charts. A thrill of pleasure ran through her. She felt she had won the argument. She looked up at Craig. He wasn't impressed.

'But the mussels are a dead end?' he said, quite deliberately changing the subject.

'I don't know,' she said frustratedly. She wished things could be easier between them, maybe if she opened up a bit, tried to show him that she really cared. 'I have a feeling that somewhere along the coastline or out in the fishing grounds the mussels may tell us a different tale.'

'There won't be much fishing for a few days, there are storms forecast.'

'I'll get them when I can . . .' she said sharply, annoyed that he seemed happiest when he could throw discouraging remarks about, as though he was determined her survey should be a failure.

'Is there anything else you wanted to talk to me about?' she snapped, looking up at him.

123

His face seemed cold and desolate, and his tight control angered her.

'No.'

'I'll get on with my work then,' she said coldly, taking up her seat, trying to ignore the pounding of her heart as she heard the door close behind him.

The following afternoon, Hope edged her way down to Grannad. The cliffs were wet and slippery after the torrential rain of the morning. She carefully eased her way down into the stormy cove, noting that the sky was still heavy and grey, the cove moody and violent. Waves crashed down frantically over the rocks, throwing up spray, flicking clumps of seaweed up into the air as though they were pancakes being tossed by an over-zealous cook.

The tide was going out, leaving a shallow channel between the shore and the over-populated little island the gulls nested on. Hope needed to collect some more mussels before the ferry left that night, and she wanted to collect them from the island. She stepped along the rocky foreshore until she reached the rocks nearest to the islands.

Even with the tide fully out, the channel was still at least a foot deep and several yards wide. She took off her boots and socks and rolled up her trouser legs. Goosepimples crept down her spine as she edged her way out into the channel. The water was deeper than she had anticipated; it came over her knees, soaking her blue cords. She paddled through the sandy-bottomed channel, feeling the current pulling her away from the island, insidiously pulling her towards the dangerous rocks of the headland.

The tiny island was full of breeding gulls, and at her approach they started to squawk, mouths gaping skywards, in a terrifying high-pitched screech. Hope put her hood up and drew on her gloves, perching in a tiny round ball on the edge of the island, her back to the birds. She stayed perfectly still for several minutes and eventually the gulls ignored her as though she was a strange coloured rock that had suddenly appeared on their territory. She edged her way slowly around the island, scraping the mussels from the rocks, little by little, trying to avoid the tacky black oil that haphazardly spattered the rocks.

And then, over the noise of the gulls, she heard a voice, calling out her name. She looked up, surprised to see Craig standing on the rocky mainland, about twenty yards away. He was shouting frantically, above the clamouring of the waves and the screeching of the gulls.

'Hope. What are you doing? The tide. Look at the tide.'

Hope looked around her. The tide had swirled in around the island. The narrow gully had become a channel, a swift-moving channel

125

of deep water, the island was fast becoming a tiny isolated outcrop of land which would be inaccessible until the next low tide.

'Here catch these.' Hope shouted, throwing the tub of mussels at him. He caught the tub and flung it down, next to her discarded boots.

'Never mind the mussels. You've got to get off there. *Now.*'

Hope looked around at the fast-moving water, the angry sea, the waves crashing violently against the black rocks. She froze.

'I can't.' Her mind and body were suddenly seized with a fear colder than the sea and the chilling wind that buffeted her legs. It ran down her spine, a cold dread, gnawing apprehension. 'I can't,' she repeated.

'Jump. Hope. *Now*. I'll pull you in. Hurry. We'll both be cut off if you don't hurry.'

'I can't!' she screamed. 'I can't move. I'm too scared,' she wailed, tears trickling down her face. It was as though all the awesome power of Grannad had suddenly been launched against her. She knew it was masterful, dominating, but she had not respected it and now it had turned its full fury on her. She heard the waves crashing against the rocks and imagined being thrown around like the seaweed, as weightless as a rag doll. All colour drained from her face and only her eyes shone out, her pupils wide and dilated, deep pools of fear.

In an instant Craig threw off his shoes and

socks, flung off his coat and jumped into the channel. The water came up to his waist, the current pulling him not towards the island, but towards the angry black rocks. He fought against the tide, clawing at the water with his hands, until he reached the island. He held out his arms.

'Come on,' he yelled impatiently, but when he saw the anguish on her face he dropped his voice to a low murmur, 'I'll look after you Hope, I'll get you back.'

She edged into his arms, feeling the freezing chill of the water engulfing her. Craig held her tight against his chest as he fought with the current. Hope cried out, feeling the relentless pull of the water. He held her ever more tightly, pressing her against his sodden body, murmuring to her in a soft low voice. He edged his way across the channel, resisting the treacherous currents, waves lapping about his chest now and breaking against his back. Hope pressed her arms tightly round him, feeling the hard muscles, the straining tension of his body. It was as though invisible threads were pulling him towards danger but he planted his feet firmly on the sand beneath him and resisted the pull of the treacherous currents. And all she knew was the seething sea, the deathly chill of the water and his grip, tight around her.

'We're safe now,' he gasped, lightening his hold on her as they reached the shoreline and he dropped Hope carefully on to the rocks before scrambling about hurriedly, collecting shoes, boots, the mussels, bundling them all up in his outstretched coat. Hope stood watching him, her mind a mesh of fear, her body shaking from head to foot, her teeth chattering, noticing the waves that had started to break on to their safe haven.

'Hurry,' he said, his breath coming in short gasps, grabbing her hand and pulling her over the rocks. 'We'll be cut off if we don't move fast.'

She dragged herself after him, her legs like jelly, starting involuntarily, tightening her grasp on Craig's hand as she saw the waves crashing before her. He led her through a tiny crevasse, taking her up, her feet cold and hurting on the sharp cliffs, until eventually they reached a high plateau, safe, dry sheltered.

He turned to her then, his face white, his eyes unreadable and as dark as the pebbles on the stormy shore, his voice tight and breathless when he spoke.

'Are you OK?'

She nodded. The words wouldn't come, her lip trembled and the tears started to fall again.

'You should never have gone out to the island. It's never safe.' His breath came in shallow gasps.

'I thought it would be all right.'

'Hope,' he said softly, 'you should have

128

asked me. I hate this cove.' He spat the words out vehemently, as though somewhere in the past Grannad had done something to hurt him. 'There's evil in this place . . . I can't explain . . . Hope . . .' He folded his arms around her and drew her to him, taking her breath away and suddenly she was tiny in his arms. 'You don't have to come here again do you?' he said in a voice that was unexpectedly soothing. Hope could feel the tension easing out of her rigid muscles as his dark tones washed over her, a gentle peace settling over her.

She shook her head. 'How did you know I was here?'

'I don't know,' he whispered softly into her hair as he tightened his grasp on her until there was just the sound of the crashing waves, the screeching seagulls and the buffeting wind all around them as they stood, united, curiously warm and still and beautiful in the purple-grey light.

'I could have drowned,' she somehow got out in a voice that clearly shook.

He loosened his hold on her, stroking his hand through her hair. 'Promise you won't do anything stupid again,' he murmured, she heard his voice resonating through his chest and she glanced up, seeing him looking down at her with dark wide eyes, his face a little flushed, his hair ruffled and wild.

'I promise.'

'We won't talk about it any more. Let's go home.'

He let her out of his arms, and he walked ahead, up the gritty cliff path, not talking and Hope sensed that he would never talk about what had happened between them again, as though none of it had ever happened at all. *Let's go home.* The words echoed around her head and suddenly she was frightened. Not of the sea, of strange violent Grannad, she was frightened of what she had seen in Craig's face. Longing, need, a vast abyss of unspoken things that lay behind his dark remote face. His last words repeated themselves in her head and her heart reached out to the dark attractive man who was still a stranger to her and she felt a deep unquenchable fear.

CHAPTER ELEVEN

She didn't understand what had happened between them on the cliffs at Grannad; she had been swept up in a tide of heady emotions. He had drawn his arms around her, taken her to him and she had felt safe, comforted, loved. And then they had drawn apart and it was like a recoil which was more powerful than the force that had drawn them together.

Now they were solemnly apart; something in his eyes, a remote expression, a glazed defensive look, kept her away from him, making her tense and uncomfortable whenever she was in his company. Days passed and the tension coiled around and through her, her mind distracted and confused whenever he was near.

She was working in the games room one night when the door opened.

'Jake's on the phone.' Craig's body had that tight business-like look to it, all tightly controlled and unattainable. 'He's waiting. Take it in my office.'

Silently, her throat tight and dry, Hope slipped past Craig and went to his office. Perched on his desk she listened to Jake's voice. The line crackled as though he were speaking whilst crunching cornflakes.

'Hope? The mussels are contaminated.

Where did you get them from? Evidence of petro-chemical pollution . . .'

The words ran round her head as she bounced back into the games room. Craig was sitting at her chair, his shiny dark hair flopped forward over his face.

'The mussels are dirty!'

She looked at him, all her inhibition forgotten in her excitement, remembering the man who had held her as though he would never let her go. It had been as though something in him had reached out to her; clinging, pulling at the heart of her; only to retreat again clam-like, inhibited, afraid, remote.

'Is that good?' he said, keeping his tone deliberately cool, turning back to the desk, pressing one of the computer keys.

'Yes! Of course! . . . What . . . what are you doing?'

'Corrections. Your spelling is terrible.'

'But you shouldn't be touching my work. It's . . . I'm not supposed . . . I—'

'OK. OK. I get the message,' he said, standing up. 'I shouldn't be looking at this. You're worried I'll go out and leak it to the press. Right?' A Californian twang in his voice deflected her attention for a moment, making her think about the man and what had made him give up his honeyed lifestyle to come back to his roots. 'You don't trust me?'

'No . . . It's not that.' She wished she could

132

look at him coldly and analytically, but every time she saw him her heart jumped, her pulses accelerated, and she felt out of control, aware only of an overwhelming need that drew her to him like a magnet, her thoughts turning back again to Grannad. She could still imagine his arms tight around her, his voice soft and low, reassuring in those warm dark tones of his.

It was her turn to speak now, and she murmured in a quiet voice so unlike her own she felt quite strange. 'I trust you with my life.'

His eyes darkened several shades at that; she stared up at him, her senses registering the electric charge in the atmosphere, her throat dry, aching with intolerable tension, her body trapped in the fierce beam of his eyes.

'Maybe I can give you some help tomorrow. There's a few things I need to do tonight,' he said as he slipped noiselessly out of the room.

An elderly widower, Archie Dundonald—a cousin to Bella Dundonald at Strainay—lived in a low stone-walled thatched cottage, near the salt marshes, to the north of Grannad, and it was to his own special brand of island hospitality that Hope was next drawn.

The salt marshes presented a terrain in total contrast to anything else Hope had seen on the island: a far-reaching expanse of grass and reeds, bog and half-submerged meadowland, mud flats and tidal pools; the darkest greens and blackest browns, until, at the wide, gaping estuary mouth, the marshland and the blue sea seeped together, fresh and saltwater, primeval life bloodbrothers.

Although it was an exposed desolate spot, there were knolls, old walls, sites of sheepfolds and a cemetery with rugged grey walls, all affording good viewpoints of the complex terrain. Hope settled, that first morning into a censusing round, moving from cemetery to knoll, to sheepfold, perching with her binoculars and telescope, entranced by the perpetual hustle and bustle of the marshland. It seethed with birdlife; courting, feeding and preening of waders, ducks, grebes, larks and buntings.

It was a mild spring day and during the course of the morning the sun rose high in the wide blue sky. She watched as a tall, burly man walked towards her, making steady progress across the boggy meadowland, his feet in heavy boots, striding out purposefully.

'My father sent me for you. It's midday.' He spoke in the quietest voice Hope had ever heard, little more than a whisper. He was a man of about forty, dark hair peppered with grey, and he had those clear blue eyes she had seen in so many of the islanders.

Hope looked up at the man and smiled, but her friendly open smile seemed to embarrass him and he looked away across the marshland, towards the reed-fringed meadowlands, waiting, as though unsure what to do next.

'Well. I'd better come then, hadn't I?' she

said breezily, packing away her telescope. Without a word he picked up her backpack, sending her thoughts momentarily to Craig, thinking of the times he had silently picked up that bag. He headed back towards the cottage which nestled in the lee of a low hill, a position which protected it from the worst ravages of the harsh north winds.

A short man, gnarled with rheumatism, stood in the doorway, boots on his feet and a blue woolly hat covering his bald pate.

'So you're the bird-counter,' he said. He narrowed his eyes. They were triangulate and clear blue, like his cousin Bella's, although his were questioning and amused, childlike and laughing.

'You've a fine head of hair, lassie, I'll say that for you,' he remarked as she lowered her hood.

She raised a brow, quizzically, looking him straight in the face, her eyes flashing a brilliant green. 'Are you always so direct?'

'Yes. Just like you girlie. Just like you. I heard you gave old Harry a good talking to, down at the quayside, over his bad manners. Always was a churlish man. He'll mind his manners the next time he sees you . . . Hope isn't it? Welcome.' He offered her a weathered hand, tanned brown and spotted with age.

'I'd heard you were a fine-looking girlie. They weren't wrong, were they son?' He turned to his son who stood speechless at his side, his eyes turned to the ground.

'Don't mind Angus. He's a quiet one. Scared of women. He's my eldest. He helps me run the farm. It'll be his when I go. The youngest ran away to sea and the daughter lives on the other side of the island with her husband and four bairns.' He stopped to draw breath and a twinkling came into his eyes. 'You survived Bella's tongue-wagging did you? And how are you getting along with Janey McClennan?' He threw back his head and laughed. It was the first time she had heard the housekeeper's Christian name. It sounded so unlike her: young and informal. 'She's a real tartar, isn't she? I can remember chasing her around the harbour, when I was a lad, running after her for a kiss.' His eyes seemed to twinkle with the memory and Hope tried to imagine the frosty woman as a girl, running, light-hearted and free, streaming over the grey cobbles of the quayside pursued by her ardent admirer.

'Did you catch her?'

'I did. For a while. And then I met Marie. Janey married a man from the mainland. They met by chance when she went to visit her sister in Aberdeen. Her parents were against the marriage. But Janey and Ian wrote to each other for nearly two years and eventually her parents gave in. He's a fisherman. So are her two sons.' Suddenly Mrs. McClennan's initial animosity made sense.

136

'There now,' he said brightly. 'That's enough of us. I want to know all about you. The winters are long and drab and you look as though you can breathe a breath of fresh air into any place you go to.'

He ushered her into the dull light of the cottage. The interior was similar to Bella's. Peat stove, armchairs on either side of the fire and the large table, set with cold meats and bread, three places laid.

'And how are you getting on with Craig?' Archie asked, a little later as they sat around the table tucking into the wholesome plain fare, a wicked twinkle in his eye.

'OK,' she said evasively, feeling heat rising up in her neck and taking a sip of her sweet black tea.

'Has he still got that wicked temper of his?' He laughed, watching the colour rising in her cheeks. 'He had a terrible temper as a boy. Still, I've a feeling you're more than a match for Craig McAllister. What say you Angus?'

Angus looked up from his plate and stared out of his gentle blue eyes, remaining silent.

'Craig's been very good over the oil business.' The old man tut-tutted, a low birdlike sound in the back of his throat and shook his head. 'The oil ruined everything. They said things would be back to normal this year. They said it was only a small spill. But the fishermen are out every hour God sends now trying to find fish and the seaweed was

137

wrecked so the crops suffer. And then there were the poor birds . . . No, Craig's been good. He'd do anything to protect the islanders.' He stared into Hope's face, screwing up his eyes to those blue triangles, dropping his voice.

'I suppose that includes giving me a hard time, does it?'

'He said he'd handle you. But I have a feeling you're more than a match for him, more than a match for him.' He shook his head and laughed.

'I don't need handling,' Hope said spikily, feeling her temper rise. 'I'm not a prize cow or a visiting dignitary. I'm a scientist and I've been sent here to do a job of work. It's as simple as that.'

Archie chuckled heartily, throwing back his head. 'Ho! Prize cow indeed! I bet the sparks fly when you two are together.'

She thought about Archie's words all afternoon. If Craig was prepared to do anything to help the islanders did that include using dirty tricks? Had he been innocently checking her spelling that night? She had begun to trust him, but maybe that was all part of his plan, maybe he would abuse that confidence, in the end.

When he picked her up that afternoon she studied him, turning over in her mind every word he spoke, noting every glance, every gesture, looking for clues. He asked her how she had got on that day and she answered

138

vaguely and he didn't question her further.

The phone was ringing as Craig and Hope returned to the hotel that night. The call was for Hope and she took it in the lobby. She hardly spoke, words choking in her throat, her face burning as she listened to the voice at the end of the line. When she finished she threw down the phone and hurtled along the corridor, storming towards Craig's office like a gale-force wind.

She burst into his office, her red hair streaming out behind her, green eyes blazing. He was sitting at his desk sipping a mug of coffee.

'Don't bother to knock.'

'That was my boss Marcus on the phone . . . he's been trying to reach me since yesterday . . .' she said breathlessly, feeling anger and pain tightening in her chest.

'Don't tell me . . . you've got a promotion,' he said in a flat tone.

'No I'm not getting a promotion. I'll be lucky if I've still got a job to go back to.'

'What's happened?'

'What's happened? What's happened? You have to ask that?'

'Yes!' He put down his mug and looked up into her face, her green eyes shining, pupils dilated, her chin defiantly thrown out, and her mouth pursed. His face was fast becoming stormy, unpredictable. 'I have to ask. What the hell is going on?'

'My mussel research has been leaked to the press. Marcus is furious. The oil company is furious. I was under strict instructions not to let any information leak out.'

'And you didn't.'

And then Craig's expression abruptly changed, his eyes becoming a blacker shade of brown. He nodded his head gently, a faint smirk growing across his lips. 'I see . . . I understand . . .' His eyes narrowed to thin slits. 'You think it was me, don't you?' he muttered in a voice that was suddenly rough.

'And wasn't it?' she said rather too shrilly.

'No. It wasn't. I gave you my word didn't I? Doesn't that mean anything to you?' Something in his voice disturbed her far more than she cared to admit. It wasn't the anger, but the sneaking pain, the disappointment underpinning his every word, and when she shot a nervous glance at him the stormy blackness of his eyes made her shudder.

'But you're the only one I told about the mussels,' she mumbled, trying to think fast.

'No I'm not. What about Jake? He knew.'

'Are you trying to tell me it wasn't you?'

'Hope.' He held his hands outstretched and he used them to emphasize every word that he spoke. 'Watch my lips. I didn't talk to the press. I didn't tell any of the islanders.'

'Then who did?'

'That's not my problem is it? Why don't you speak to Jake?'

140

'But he couldn't . . . he wouldn't—'

'You'd much rather believe I was the culprit, wouldn't you?'

'I'm sorry . . .' she knew at that moment she had made a terrible mistake. 'I didn't think . . . I shouldn't have jumped to conclusions . . . I'm sorry . . . and don't tell me my apologies come too easily. I'm truly sorry.' Her voice had a shrill edge to it now, faltering, near tears. 'Do you understand?'

She looked up, her eyes glazed by tears and then she rushed from the room, hurtling up the stairs, not stopping until she had flung herself down on the bed. Tears rained down on her pillow. Why was she always jumping to the wrong conclusion, assuming, even now, after all he had done, that Craig McAllister would do anything to betray her? It was as though she needed to think of him as an enemy, as though that was the only way she could keep herself at a distance from him. It would be impossible to fall in love with your enemy.

She didn't hear him tap lightly on her door, nor hear his footsteps as he stepped across her room. And then he was sitting at her side, and his hand was stroking her head, gently pushing the tendrils of hair from her wet face.

'Hey. Stop it,' he murmured throatily. 'I'd probably have made the same mistake if I'd been in your shoes. Forget about it.' His warm fingers stroked her face, coaxing her heartbeat

141

to a slower but more insistent tattoo, his touch sending heat coursing through her body.

'I'm such a fool. I make such a mess of things.'

'No you're not. You're doing a great job. Working all the hours God sends to get this impossible survey done. Forget about it. We won't talk about it any more.'

'That's what you always say.'

'What?'

'*We won't talk about it any more,*' she murmured thinking back to that moment on the cliffs at Grannad.

He stooped over her, and dropped a light kiss on her cheek. She was aware of the clean male scent of his body, his chest brushing against her breast. Her heart was beating a wild crazy tattoo and she felt sure he must hear it and know the fevered thoughts that were rushing through her mind.

'Why don't you get an early night?' he said in a brotherly tone. 'You're exhausted. I'll switch off the computer.' He stroked his hand along her arm and then stood up. She turned, watching as he walked out of her room.

She slept the heavy drugged sleep that always came to her when she had been crying and when she woke in the morning her cheek burned with the memory of his kiss.

CHAPTER TWELVE

Hope looked up from her steaming mug of black tea, her eyes settling on Archie Dundonald as he prodded life back into his black-bowled pipe. This was her third visit to Archie's. She looked forward to his company as much as he looked forward to hers. He was an amusing lively man and in many ways he reminded her of her grandfather, always questioning, always full of fun, like a child who had never grown up.

'So,' Archie drawled, leaning back on his chair. 'Do you have any brothers or sisters?'

'No.'

The door opened. Craig entered the cottage, his dark shining hair wind-tousled and dampened, spots of rain spattering his coat. Warmth flooded over Hope, followed in its wake by a cold wave of unknown fear. She felt constrained, iron-clad, confused, she never knew what to do when he made her feel this way.

'Good day, Craig,' Archie said effusively. 'Come in and sit down.'

'No. I won't stop. I've just come to borrow a peat shovel. I'm over at the McGregors'—'

'Sit down, lad. Have some tea,' he insisted. He produced a mug and poured some of the dark treacly tea into it. Craig stole a quick glance at Hope, she felt herself colour and she hurriedly looked away. 'Sit down,' Archie commanded, pointing to a chair. 'You may as well shelter out of the rain.' The sky had darkened and Hope noticed the soft rain pattering against the window pane.

Silently Craig sat down, his body held as if in a tight coil.

'Hope was just telling me that she's an only child, weren't you Hope?'

Hope felt herself colour under the fine scrutiny of Craig's dark eyes. She nodded, feeling flustered and uncomfortable.

'Used to getting your own way, I suppose?' He laughed and looked across at Craig and then he laughed again.

'I can't understand why a lovely girl like you isn't married. Twenty seven! I'd have thought some young man would have snapped you up years ago.'

'There's more to life than walking up the aisle with the first man who happens along, Archie!' Hope tried to keep her voice level and light-hearted but it sounded terse and false.

Hope felt colour filling her cheeks. When she was alone with Archie she enjoyed his directness and she played him at his own game. But now that Craig was here she felt awkward and off-balance and unable to respond. His presence seemed to change everything for her wherever she was.

144

'Not even engaged?'

'No!'

'No one special?'

'No!' A fleeting image of Roger passed through her mind. She'd had time to think about him. She'd reached a decision about their relationship.

'What do you think Craig?'

'I think Hope probably knows her own mind.' His voice exerted a curious power over her, it was soft and soothing, and she felt her body melting, drowning in his deep tones. She was falling, falling under a spell, entrapped, enchanted and then suddenly she caught herself, shocking herself back to her senses like someone jerked back to consciousness after a dream of falling.

'And I think you're a nosey old man, Angus Dundonald,' said Hope breezily, aware of a silly quaver in her voice. She stood up. The chair scraped on the flagstone floor and Hope's nerves grated. She walked over towards the sink.

'I'll do those dishes Hope. You did them yesterday and you shouldn't have.' He turned to Craig. 'She's good company, isn't she Craig? She's been telling me all about the place she's from. The Dovey estuary in Wales. Sounds a lovely place, doesn't it?'

Craig snatched a quick glance at her before he spoke. 'I'll have to ask Hope to tell me about it sometime.'

145

Hope felt her temperature rise. She stepped across to her backpack, kneeling down and fussing around with it, shielding her face from the men until she felt the colour in her cheeks subside. 'I'll be off then. 'Bye Archie. Thanks for lunch. Look after yourself.'

' 'Bye Hope. And don't give this young fellow here too much of a hard time, will you?'

Hope managed a wan smile and stepped out of the door. Something warned her that Craig was behind her.

'Hope.'

She looked around and his eyes seem to fix on her in a deeply disturbing way.

'I'll be working over the hill at the McGregors'. If it comes on to rain just pack up and come on over and we'll clear off home.' Hope wondered if he realized he always spoke of the hotel as home now when they were together.

She looked up at him. He was wearing dark brown cords and a cream cable jumper that seemed to bring out the dark of his eyes, his beard and hair.

'I owe you an apology,' she said. 'It was Jake who leaked all that information. He happened to mention it to a friend of his, who then happened to mention it to a journalist friend of his.' She squirmed inside, waiting for his response, expecting some cutting remark; it was little more than she deserved and his dark gaze settled on her, making her heart beat out

146

of time.

'Let's forget about it.' He smiled softly. His hands were peat-stained and suddenly she recalled something she had said when they had first met and now the memory of her words burned in her, shaming her to speak again.

'I was wrong about something else.'

'I don't think so,' Craig said softly.

'When we first met . . .' She looked up and then away, out across the salt marsh, listening to the clear cry of a lark high up in the sky. 'I made a facetious remark about your hands— not doing manual work.'

He looked down at his stained hands and smiled. 'I remember . . . those hands never go near peat bog or—'

'Don't,' Hope pleaded, feeling her insides squirm at the memory.

His smile broadened. 'You were half-right. I don't do any manual work in the winter. It's now, Spring, when I help out. Cutting peat. That sort of thing.'

'I seem to spend my life apologizing to you.'

'You don't have to,' he said in a soft lingering voice, his words subtly ambiguous. For some reason that gentle tone struck a painfully raw nerve. She actually quivered as if he had touched her.

'I'd better get back to work,' Hope said, feeling a desperate need to be out of his company.

'Maybe we could eat together tonight,' he

147

murmured, lowering his voice still more. 'I don't have to go out. I'll ask Mrs. McClennan. Yes?'

Hope nodded, her voice locked in her throat like a furled knot. The afternoon passed in a daze, and later, when they drove back to the hotel she found that she couldn't concentrate on anything that was said. Her own words seemed to be spoken as if from a long distance, she felt disembodied, enchanted, her mind flitting on to a distant horizon.

She didn't know what she wanted from Craig. When she was away from him she tried to think of him in clear clinical terms. He was her host, he drove her about, he corrected her work for her. But when she saw him, something in her melted and yearned for him, calling out to be touched, stroked, to be cherished and loved by him. It was an enveloping feeling, a beautiful sensation and she fought hard against it.

Being here on the island, away from London, she'd had time to think. She realized it was pointless going on seeing Roger. He obviously saw marriage as the inevitable end result of their relationship. Sometimes, in the past, she had told herself that maybe she could be happy with Roger, that love might flower. But now she knew that was all illusory. She could never feel anything more than gentle, almost sisterly affection for him and she would tell him so when she returned to London.

She knew that there could never be any future in a relationship with Craig. But he had awakened feelings, deep, unknown stirring sensations in her and she would never be able to settle for second-best.

She had brought one dress with her to the island: a deep emerald-green dress, a fine sheath of cashmere which clung to her figure and brought out the natural brilliance of her eyes. It had a high cowl neckline which seemed to emphasise the fine line of her neck and it was clipped in tightly at the waist, calling attention to her slim waist and subtly curving hips. She slipped her feet into the only truly glamorous item she had brought to the island: a pair of black strappy high-heels. She brushed her hair until it shone, stroked beige eyeshadow on her lids, mascara on her lashes and highlighted her lips with the perfect shade of red. She stood for a moment, looking at the face in the mirror, trying to match up the face with the thoughts racing through her mind, wondering why it was becoming impossible to get Craig McAllister out of her mind.

How could she want to be in the company of a man who was so deeply disturbing? He set every cell, every fibre, every muscle of her body on edge whenever he was near. She fought a constant struggle to keep her mind on an even keel when they were together. And yet, when they were apart, she felt a sense of

149

loss, of deep welling emptiness, as though she wasn't really alive until he was close. Her cheeks burned in anticipation, and as she stepped down the stairs she felt strangely excited and enlivened, half-fearful, half-yearning.

She had almost reached the bottom of the stairs when she heard his office door open. Craig stepped out and Hope gasped. He was dressed in a suit, it was grey with a fine blue fleck running through it, his shirt was purest white, starched crisp, his tie a contrasting blue. The clothes were not the biggest change. His face had been shaved clean. He no longer possessed the dark intimidating beard and now Hope could see that there was a fine line to his cheek-bones and that his square chin had a tiny cleft in it. He had been an attractive man before, but now, now it was different, now she was lost. Her heart seemed to thunder and she felt colour rushing into her face, rushing to the roots of her hair.

'I . . .' she faltered. 'You look so different without the beard,' she managed, aware that his dark appraising glance was running over her.

'It's a winter beard. I always shave it off when the spring comes.'

'Oh. I see,' Hope said vacantly, hardly aware of what she was saying, unable to take her eyes from him, aware of the animalistic power beneath his sophisticated veneer.

Neither of them spoke. She looked up at him with huge green eyes and was frightened at the deep longing that she saw in his eyes.

'You look beautiful,' his voice seemed to sound in her somewhere where she was powerless against it. 'I think you're very beautiful.' His words seemed to reverberate around her, exerting a curious power over her, making her feel relaxed and wildly alert at the same time.

'Dinner's ready.' Mrs. McClennan looked out of the dining-room. Craig stole a brief glance at Hope, his eyes still full of that deep yearning, and then he lightly touched her elbow, directing her softly towards the dining-room.

'Now there's a pretty sight,' said Mrs. McClennan, her eyes lighting up. Her gaze passed from Craig to Hope and then back again, all the while a smile broadening on her lips, a twinkling appearing in her eyes.

All through dinner Hope was aware of his eyes on her, drawing her out, touching something deep inside her, seeking out the very heart of her. Mrs. McClennan had produced a fine meal—smoked salmon, local roast beef and one of her special trifles with oodles of cream—but Hope hardly tasted the food, the meal passed in a daze.

'Shall we go to my office and have some brandy?' Craig asked as they sipped their coffee, in a voice that was unusually husky.

'I . . .' Caution told her to say no. 'I don't drink brandy.' It was true.

'I have some other liqueurs. There's sure to be one I can tempt you with.' He stood up, his dark eyes washing over her and all her resistance was gone.

There was a peat fire in Craig's office. It burned with the same red flame Hope had seen that first time, out at Bella's. She sipped her orange liqueur, feeling the spirit burn the back of her throat, glad almost to feel sensation, anything other than the strange turmoil that whipped around her mind making her feel enslaved and out of control. They sat in the leather armchairs, on either side of the fire. Silence fell over the room like a heavy cloying shroud. She felt his eyes on her and she burned with the knowledge.

'Could you take me up towards the north coast tomorrow?' She didn't want to talk about work, but somehow she had to break the silence.

'Yes. Of course.'

'I want to check up on the seals and the puffins for a few days.'

'You can go to my cottage. It's on the coast. It would be perfect for you.'

She faltered, feeling her cheeks burn, unsure what he was suggesting. He seemed to sense her unease as though he was reading her mind.

'I won't be there. I'm helping at the

McGregors'. I could take you up there in the morning. Set the peat fire. The weather's going to be showery over the next few days so you'll be able to dodge the rain.'

He made it all sound so appealing. How could she turn him down? And yet, a little voice inside her told her that she should refuse. But she was running out of time. She still had to survey the seals and puffins and go out with the fishermen. 'I'll use it. Thank you.'

Silence fell over the room again. Hope took another sip of liqueur, concentrating on the burning at the back of her throat.

'You'll be gone soon. Back to London,' he said, putting all that strange soothing softness into his voice again.

'Yes,' she mumbled, feeling a knot in her throat.

'Perhaps we could meet for dinner, or something.' He paused looking at her, his eyes suddenly gleaming in that highly disturbing way. 'Next time I'm in London.' Something in his voice disturbed her far more than she cared to admit. Although he had kept his voice deliberately light, she had the feeling that he meant every word of it, he had no intention of letting her vanish from his life.

'Yes,' Hope got out, in a frightened rasp. She felt as though she was rushing out of control, aware only of the highly disturbing, deeply attractive male. She felt fear. But it wasn't fear of him. It was fear of herself. Fear of what she might say or do if she didn't keep a tight rein on her emotions, they were like horses held tightly in harness, straining to be away, to be free.

'Look.' She could hear a slightly desperate tone in her voice and that frightened her too. She stood up. 'I'm rather tired. Perhaps I'd better go to bed . . . to sleep . . . I.' Words tumbled out in a meaningless jumble.

He stood up and stepped towards her, touching her arm. His touch incited a fierce heat in her veins. Her breath caught in her throat, she was lost. Gently, soothingly, his voice a low coaxing murmur, he turned her towards him, calling out her name. And when she stood before him he lifted up her chin towards him and she didn't know whether she saw or imagined him lower his head. She closed her eyes, and then his lips met hers. The lightest, gentlest of pressures, her skin pulsed beneath her mouth and her lips parted, welcoming him into their warm sensuality, his tongue darting in soft recesses, moist channels. She felt his arms tight about her, his long lean body hard against her and she knew she was powerless.

'Hope,' he murmured, his mouth peppering her neck and throat with kisses. 'I want you.' She knew only the strong male virility of him, sensed his longing and she felt out of her depth. She seemed to be hurtling out of control. And then she thought of Roger. She needed to tell Craig about Roger. Explain that he meant nothing to her.

'Craig,' she whispered. His arms were snaked about her, his kisses plundering her neck. 'There's something I need to tell you.'

Her words had an ominous ring to them. She felt him tense. He drew away from her. 'Go on.'

'I have a boyfriend.'

'I see.'

'He doesn't mean anything to me.'

'Naturally. You're hundreds of miles from him.'

'No. You don't understand. I'm going to tell him when I go back . . . tell him it's over.'

'No you're not.' His voice had a horribly cynical chill to it. 'You'll go back to London. Resume your London life. God, what a fool I've been. To think. After everything that happened before.'

She touched him, gently, she wanted to soothe him, make him understand that she wasn't the person he thought she was, but he stiffened under her light touch, his hand bone-white and tense and she retreated, a hooded look of pain and humiliation in her brilliant green eyes.

'Well. You got what you wanted.' His voice was a cruel cynical chill.

'What do you mean?'

'The cottage. For your survey. It was well worth the trouble you took, wasn't it?'

155

'I don't understand . . .'

'You obviously went to a lot of trouble, your dress, your hair . . . and of course it had the desired effect . . . I was like putty in your hands.'

'It wasn't like that.' Hope screamed out. 'You must believe me.'

His head reared back, his chest heaving in a harsh intake of breath, his dark eyes glittering in the sombre light of the room. His eyes raked over her, her swollen mouth, her huge and dilated green eyes.

'No, Hope. I don't have to believe you at all. I don't know what the pay-off is but whatever Sir Gregory's giving you it's worth every penny.'

'I'm not getting any pay-off. Can't you get that through your thick skull?'

He never responded to her when she was outraged and in pain; something in him cut off. He stared at her then, with icy dark eyes and Hope trembled at the contempt writ large on his face.

'I'll take you out to the cottage tomorrow. You can stay there for a few days if you like. Then you won't have to see me at all.'

'If that's what you want.'

'Want? What I want? What has that got to do with anything?' He opened the door. 'I'm going out. Be ready at nine tomorrow.'

'Where are you going . . . be careful . . .' she muttered, her voice shrill and desperate.

She threw up her head in a quick agonised little gesture of pain that seemed to enrage him even more and he said, 'Don't worry. I'm not about to throw myself off the nearest cliff, if that's what you're worried about . . . and I won't be touching the car . . . after all, you'll be needing a taxi-driver tomorrow, won't you?' he finished cynically, his eyes as black as the night and as stormy as his mood.

CHAPTER THIRTEEN

Sitting out on the black cliffs below Craig's cottage it was easy for Hope to be lulled into contemplation. The sea slapped against the rocks and the seals gathered close by, basking languorously, watching her with their big solemn eyes.

In life it seemed there were few moments of clarity, but here on Branaigg, the sky high and wide, lulled by the rhythmic pounding of the waves on the jagged black rocks below, Hope had a momentary vision, clear and bright.

She suddenly felt part of it all. Connected. And the world she had left behind, her London life seemed vacuous and superficial, a dull tinkling of bells, dissonant and unattractive. She had changed. Branaigg had changed her. With knife-sharp insight she realized it would be impossible to simply resume her former life. If she did so she would always be aware of a dull ache, a longing. Island sights and sounds were fixed forever in her mind: the bays, the birds, the waves, the sound of the wind rustling through the marron grass or a lone curlew out on the marshlands. Branaigg had insinuated its way into her consciousness and she knew it would always be there.

She recalled as a teenager feeling a similar

sense of joy, as she tramped along the Dovey estuary, at the break of day or at sunset when the flaming rays of the sun sank low in the sky. But Branaigg had a magical air about it from morning till night and it had seeped into her every pore. Every step, night, morning, amongst sand dunes or out on rocky headland, it all seemed to bring that heady sense of exhilaration.

The long hours should have been exhausting her, but in fact she felt enlivened by the work and her face had a rosy, healthy glow to it, far different from the unhealthy winter pallor she had brought with her from London.

But the harmony she felt with nature was in complete contrast to the raging turmoil of feelings she felt towards Craig. She told herself he meant nothing to her. But why did she torment herself by recalling how he had kissed her, his arms locked about her, as though he would never let her out of his grasp? If she closed her eyes she could still relive the burning sensation she had felt wherever he had touched her.

At the end of the day, still confused and dismayed, Hope tramped back to Craig's cottage. She stopped when she saw his car. Her stomach clenched. As she walked in the door she spotted him crouched in front of the peat wove, the material of his black cords pulled tight against his lean muscular legs.

'What . . . what are you doing here?' she

faltered.

'Checking up on you . . .' He glanced up at her and caught the confused look in her brilliant green eyes. 'Mrs. McClennan thought you might have trouble with the stove, it is a bit temperamental, so she asked me to come and check.'

'She needn't have asked you.'

He was making sure she appreciated he was only there because Mrs. McClennan had asked him. She wondered why he had bothered to come at all. Hope didn't know what she felt, seeing him there, it awoke too many confusing sensations in her, stimulating a fear of her stirring unknown emotions.

He had the door of the stove wide open. In Bella's kitchen the peats had burned to a glowing living red, but here the fire was hardly smoking.

He tut-tutted in a way that reminded her of Archie Dundonald. 'You'd never make an island wife!' It was a careless, throwaway remark.

'No one's likely to ask me,' she replied drolly.

He turned to her then and threw her an ugly look, his face distorted as if with a secret pain. But then his face became a remote mask and when he spoke again there was a cynical edge to his harsh voice. 'Still. You won't have to worry about peat stoves and bird counts and seals for much longer. You'll be back in

160

London. Back where you belong.'

'What makes you so sure it's where I belong?'

'Well this desolate island isn't exactly your scene, is it?'

'How do you know? You've never asked me.'

'I imagined it was a foregone conclusion you hated the place . . . after all,' he said cruelly, recalling her words that first day on the quayside, 'it's hardly paradise.'

'Well you're wrong. I do love London. It's frenetic, vibrant, alive. But I could never love London the way I love Branaigg.' She felt her cheeks reddening at her frankness. She wondered whether she had said too much. She'd been so careful, so reserved up till now. But what did it matter? She'd be gone soon. He might as well know her true feelings. 'This island is magical, it's special. The people are too. Even Mrs. McClennan has a heart of gold underneath all that toughness. And I'm going to miss this place when I go.'

Tears welled up, making her green eyes seem even more startling in the dull evening light of the cottage. 'Satisfied?' she managed through her tears, not even trying to hide the tremor in her voice. And then she rushed from the room, to the bedroom, hardly thinking what she was doing, only knowing that she had to be out of his company, out of his sight.

She rushed over to the window and pressed

her head down so it rested on the cool slate sill. Hot tears rained down on her hands. And then she felt his hand on her shoulder.

'Hope . . . Hope.' His voice was warm and soothing, reaching deep inside her. With firm hands on her shoulders he turned her towards him. 'Hope,' he repeated and the sound of her name on his lips ran around her head. He ran a finger down her tearful face, catching warm salty tears, stroking her face dry.

'Hope. I'm going to miss you.' His voice was all warm dark tones and she was helpless, lost. He pulled her towards him and she felt her tears dampening his shirt, sensed his strong lean chest and heard his heart beating out its regular tattoo, calming her, soothing her to a gentler pace.

'I'm going to miss you too,' she offered. 'I don't know why . . . I don't understand . . .'

He pulled her chin up and dropped his mouth on hers like a stone. His lips were warm and comforting and yet there was a strong virile edge to him, barely concealed masculinity, and Hope felt fright, alone with him in the cottage. She hardly knew anything of him. He pressed her lips apart. He did it with a silent concentration that was completely unnerving and then she responded with a shudder and was kissing him back. She heard his sharp intake of breath at her response as she gave in and slid her arms around his back. His head angled down as he bent her back further and he nuzzled underneath her hair to kiss her neck and then to suck gently at the pulse beating in her ears.

'Why did you come back to Branaigg?' she asked him, her voice against his chest.

'I came back because I felt dislocated, empty, drifting. I'd lived in California for too long, been sucked into the easy lifestyle, the warm cocoon of superficiality. I had to find my roots again. Begin to feel real feelings again. Good honest feelings. I wanted to see huge breakers, white sand, the desolate saltmarshes. I came back and Branaigg healed me. And then the oil came and I stayed. I had to protect Branaigg the way it had protected me.'

'And that's all?'

For a moment, and only for a moment, something desolate and terrible looked out of those exquisite dark eyes. He stroked a finger along her neck, it was a teasing, tantalizing sensation and when she looked into his face again she saw the glitter of intent in his eyes and heat bolted through her body.

'There's nothing else you need to know.' His voice had a slight edge to it again. 'When you tell me that you love Branaigg I understand how you feel.'

'The island's returning to normal Craig. The bird counts, the breeding figures, even the seal numbers, it's all encouraging news.'

He pulled away from her. 'Is this your way of telling me that the report won't be favourable?'

'No. That's not what I'm saying at all.' Why did things swing out of control whenever they were together? One moment they were close, as though their hearts were beating as one. The next moment the battle lines were drawn and all affection had been withdrawn. Her voice had that cold clinical edge to it now, she always reacted this way when he attacked her. She knew it angered him, she could sense his temper rising, it made her breath catch in her throat, but somehow she couldn't stop herself. 'The mussels from Grannad were oily, but the ones from Strainay were clean, it's not really conclusive evidence. That's the facts.'

'The facts,' he repeated caustically. 'The facts are all that matters, aren't they?'

'I haven't finished my work yet. Sir Gregory said he was quite prepared to let me do the mussel research as long as I completed the census work.'

'Don't give me that. You've already made up your mind.'

'No I haven't. Don't you trust me?'

He said nothing, his mouth pursed.

'Don't you trust me?' she repeated, hating the desperate tone to her voice. 'After all we've been through together?'

'Exactly what have we been through together? We've dined together. I've played taxi-driver to you . . . and don't forget spelling checker . . . and I rescued you from the mighty sea.'

'It's more than that.' She had nothing to lose now. She might be making a complete fool of herself but she didn't care any more. She couldn't go on, like Craig, hiding from what was going on between them, pretending that they felt nothing for each other.

'Oh yes,' he carped cynically, his dark eyes pinning her with their coolly mocking gaze. 'I'm forgetting a few kisses, here and there, a few very pleasant embraces. Something to while away the tedious hours whilst marooned on this bleak island. Nothing particularly memorable to a sophisticated girl like you.'

Anger burned through her. He had taken everything, everything that was good and true and real and reduced it to a few cynical comments. He had taken the goodness from it all. Her throat was a tight furled knot.

She felt defenceless against his attack and then, the anger boiled up in her anew and she lifted a hand, to strike him across the face. But he had sensed her intention and he caught her hand, pinning it painfully in mid-air.

'Oh no you don't. You see . . . you can't even keep your promises, can you?' She looked at him with a puzzled frown. 'Remember that night I found you walking alone outside? You hit me then. You gave me your promise that you'd never do it again. Your promises are like all the rest of you, aren't they? Superficial. Without substance.'

165

'Why do you love being angry with me? Is it me you're really angry at? Or is it someone else?'

'I don't know what you're talking about.'

'Don't you? I know that whenever we are close you draw away from me as though I was a poisonous snake about to strike.'

'You want me to be close do you? You've been missing intimate contact have you? Well . . . you have been here nearly three weeks now . . . you must be feeling very frustrated.' He reached for her arms and turned her, forcing her towards the bed, throwing her on to it and dropping down beside her, his body heavy, making her feel claustrophobic, trapped. He started to pull at her jumper, his hands reaching inside, touching her warm flesh. 'Is this what you want?' She could feel him breathing hard and deep, his body as tight and strong as steel. Panic and pain tore at her with knife-sharp claws as a wild trembling coursed through her.

'No,' she screamed out, her heart slamming in thick hard strokes. She was lost. They were miles away from the nearest cottage. There was no one here to help her, no one could save her.

The sound of her voice hit a raw nerve in Craig and he loosened his hold on her and straightened her jumper, his eyes bearing into her like solemn lost souls of the night, a heart-wrenching mix of despair and contempt.

166

He stood up, running a hand through his shiny conker-brown hair. His face was blanched, his eyes standing out like wide dark pebbles. All the anger had ebbed away from him and when he spoke again his voice had that soft soothing quality to it that made Hope want to reach out to him.

'I'm sorry. I'd better go. I think I'll walk first and then come back for the car. I won't bother you any more.'

She tried to calm the trembling that coursed through her body. She watched as he left the cottage, studying that long elegant stride of his, knowing that everything between them was finished now. There was nothing left. It had all been used up, distorted into an ugly new image and she needed to turn away from him now and forget that he had ever existed. It would be the only way. She could not feel safe when he was close by.

He hadn't returned by the time she went to bed. Hope felt afraid to sleep. He might burst into the cottage, his cottage, at any moment and she would be defenceless against him. But in the end sleep overtook her, a deep dreamless sleep that rendered her oblivious to any sound around her: the sound of crashing waves, a car starting, the cottage door opening, footsteps around her. When she woke up in the morning the light was streaming in through the bedroom window. She sat up and looked down at the heavy counterpane. It was a gold satin eiderdown. It hadn't been on the bed when she went to sleep last night. Had she put it on in the night? There was no memory. She felt confused. She got out of bed, puffing her robe around her. As she walked into the main room, she was shocked at the sight which greeted her.

Sprawled out in an armchair by the peat stove was Craig, his eyes closed, his head bowed, his face lined with a great tiredness, the firm mouth set. Hope walked gingerly towards him. His hair was casually ruffled. In the harsh morning light his face was deathly pale. She looked at his chest, her own heart bolting within her; it didn't seem to be moving. She touched his face. It was the first time she had ever stroked his skin. His cheeks were rough with purplish bristles, but the skin close to his ears was baby soft and warm. And then she detected the faint sound of his breath.

He opened his eyes. Her hand jerked back as if burned, her face flooding with an appalled realization as his face came vividly alive, his dark eyes leaping. Everything had been in her face in that instance, forgiveness, uncertainty, naked yearning and new flooding tenderness.

'Morning,' he said softly and his voice seemed to be in her blood. She pulled away from him and stood up.

'I wasn't sure . . .'

He looked at her, and a light of

appreciation lit up his eyes. 'I had a puncture, just along the road. It was too dark to change the wheel so I had to come back here.' He dropped his glance, not meeting hers as though suddenly remembering what had happened between them and feeling ashamed.

'Did you put that eiderdown over me?'

He nodded. 'It gets chilly in the middle of the night. You wouldn't have been warm enough.'

'You've slept all night with no cover.'

He yawned and stood up, spreading out his arms. He seemed even taller and more powerful with his arms outstretched. 'It's warm here by the stove. It's working properly now. I'll be off.'

'Would you like some coffee? Or something to eat before you go?'

His gaze fell over the curve of her breast and the fine line of her hips. He shook his head. 'And you want me to pick you up tomorrow?'

'Yes. Please.'

'You'll be all right till then?' There was a touch of concern in his voice and she heard it.

'Yes. I'll be fine,' she said, trying to sound cool and composed although her heart was thundering in her chest.

'Of course. I was forgetting.' His voice had that cynical chill to it Hope had grown to loathe. 'You survived the rainforests of Indonesia, didn't you? This is nothing to you.'

He marched out of the cottage before Hope had a chance to respond. But what could she say anyway? She had grown weary of their skirmishes. She had now given up any thought that they might resolve their differences.

It was as though every remark she ever made always stood between them. Sooner or later it was thrown up between them, another weapon, more ammunition for the continuing war. She shuddered when she remembered that she had told him that she loved the island. How would he twist those words against her? It seemed as though the more they spoke to each other the more they drew apart. As though they spoke totally different languages. The ultimate culture clash. Perhaps, in the end she would be glad to be back in London. She couldn't take this emotional warfare any longer.

CHAPTER FOURTEEN

'Do you want me to come with you?' Craig asked flatly, as he stopped the car on the quayside the next day.

'No thanks. I'll arrange the fishing trips myself,' Hope said spikily, determined not to be dependent on Craig's solicitations.

Hope stomped over the grey cobbles. Fishermen were busy on the quayside. Memories of that first morning came flooding back to her, and when she saw the stocky grey-haired fisherman walking towards her, her stomach clenched in fear, she knew she couldn't face any more hostility.

'Hope isn't it?' He extended a strong tanned hand and smiled. 'I'm Harry. Craig tells us you want to go out with the fishing boats.'

'Yes . . .' The mention of Craig's name threw her off key. 'Yes . . . I don't know . . .' she faltered.

'Don't worry. It's all been arranged. Craig sorted it out. Ian McClennan will take you out. He asked me to give you a message. Said be down here at eight tomorrow morning . . . oh . . . and,' he looked at her kindly and added, 'wear something warm. It can be mighty chilly out there.'

Her relief at not having encountered any hostility was immediately replaced by fury as she stormed back to the car. She supposed she should feel grateful that Craig McAllister had deigned to smooth her path for her. But she didn't, she simply felt furious that he had interfered in her life again without her consent.

'Thanks!' she said disparagingly as she slipped back into her seat.

'My pleasure,' he responded sarcastically.

She whipped around to glare at him, her eyes blazing. 'I *am* quite capable of arranging a few fishing trips myself.' She started to shake, she hadn't known he could anger her so, he took her emotions to a higher plane every time she saw him. She turned away and looked out of the window, her eyes unseeing, only aware of the stormy emotions raging through every cell of her body. 'Why can't you keep your nose out of my affairs?'

'Because I . . .' His voice trailed off, curiously.

'What?' Hope snapped.

'Nothing.'

He turned the key in the ignition and drove up the hill and out of Castlebay.

A little later that morning, Hope hurtled along the hotel corridor, her arms laden with papers and maps. Too late she saw Craig as he backed out of his office. Swinging around he crashed right into her, knocking her papers flying. Hope reeled backwards and he grabbed her as she very nearly fell, jerking her up

172

towards him.

'Why don't you look where you're going?' she spat out.

'Why don't you wear a warning bell?'

'You mean like one of those Swiss cows?' she cracked. Suddenly the feel of his hands sent alarming shimmers coursing through her body. 'Why don't you . . .' she began, but the words suddenly evaporated, her throat had become a tight furled knot and she felt suddenly breathless.

His eyes contracted to dark slits. The harshness slipped from his voice and when he spoke his voice was full of soothing gentle tones that touched her somewhere deep inside.

'Why don't I what, Hope?'

She hadn't wanted it to happen, hadn't wanted to feel it. To feel that longing oozing through every cell of her body, from the tips of her toes to the top of her head. But the way he looked at her released a strange new chain of reactions, gloriously warm, brave new and feverish waves of sensation. She took a deep breath and when she spoke there was an unfamiliar huskiness to her voice. 'Why don't you let me kiss you?'

She leaned forward and approached him. He drew her closer to him and his arms snaked around her back until she could only feel his arms tight around her back and his chest pressing against her tight swollen breasts. A

173

desperate urgency seemed to translate itself from their touch and their lips met in a hungry passionate kiss. And then she drew away from Craig, but he held her, keeping her close. Together, utterly still for a moment, his arms still tight about her, her hands to his shoulders for balance. She looked up into his eyes. She could have drowned in those depths.

He pushed open his office door, pulling Hope into his room and closing the door after him, he pressed her urgently against the closed door. She felt the warmth under his checked shirt, his tight breathing, that lean body flush with hers. He dropped his mouth on hers, his tongue tracing its way into the moist recesses of her mouth.

His arms tightened around her and she gasped, half moaning for breath. His hands moved to her waist, loosening the shirt from her trousers and suddenly his arms were caressing the warm skin of her back. She moaned involuntarily, her senses lost to the shuddering warmth and wonder of it all. His hands moved from her back, loosening the buttons of her shirt. And she felt his slim long-fingered hands on her full aching breasts, all the while his lips trailing kisses along her neck.

'Craig,' she whispered against the rough skin of his cheek. 'I don't know what to do . . . I have to go soon . . . back to London . . .'

'We'll meet. In London. But now. We have to talk. I can't get you out of my mind.' He

174

squeezed her tight and groaned. She felt the sound reverberating through his lean chest. 'We need to spend some time together. Over the next few days.'

'Don't forget I'm going out for the mussels.'

'I don't want you to go.'

'I have to.'

'No you don't.'

'I do. The mussels are essential.'

'Let the men collect them.'

'I can't.'

'You don't trust them?'

'It's not that. I've got to map it all. Do it all. It's my report.'

'I don't want you to go.'

An ugly silence fell over the room and now his arms on her shoulders felt like constraints, manacles, as though he was trying to intimidate her in some way.

'Why don't you want me to go? What are you afraid of?' she asked, aware of a silly quaver in her voice, looking up at him and seeing his face dark and remote.

'What *is* your pay-off?'

She looked up at him, hardly believing his words and as he saw the expression of bitter distaste flood her face, he smiled without humour.

'Surely you're not afraid I'm going to find out that there is no long-term pollution?'

'My God! Why do you think I've made such a fuss about the fishing?'

'Presumably because you believe there is a problem.'

'Exactly.'

'Then what are you afraid of?'

'Nothing. Little environmental scientist. Nothing at all.' His voice was scathing. Everything was over between them. He obviously didn't trust her. What other reason could he have for trying to prevent her from going out on the fishing boat? Now her anger was laced with bitterness and when she spoke her voice was cold and detached, distant from her as though someone else was talking, not her.

'Maybe you needed a cause. Somewhere to direct your energies. Coming back here after the high life in Hollywood must have been something of a shock.'

She rued the rash words. She wanted to claw them back as soon as they were out of her mouth. They seemed to hang in the air between them for endless seconds and her pulse did a panicky jig at the stormy glint of anger and hurt in his eyes.

'So this has all been a form of psychotherapy for me, has it?'

Every muscle in her body tensed to screaming point. Things had got out of hand again and suddenly there was no going back.

'You tell me,' she said cynically, hating the sound of her voice.

'Get back to your survey, Miss

Environmental Scientist. Leave the psychology to someone else. Human feelings really aren't your forte.'

He pulled away from her and looked down at her dishevelled appearance, her cheeks love-flushed, her hair awry and her shirt unbuttoned, her breasts half-revealed. Disgust laced his eyes as his lip furled.

'Go on. *Go*. Why did I ever kid myself that there might be a future for us?' Her hands were shaking as she tried to fasten the buttons of her shirt. 'I can't take this any more. Being near you. It's destroying me. I'm going away.' She looked up at that, pain etched across her features. 'I'll go up to the cottage. Till you go. Then we won't need to meet, or talk or feel anything any more.'

Hope fled to her room and the tears flowed. Things between them became more awful every time they met, but now they had reached the end. It was as though the urgency she felt between them, the desperate need, the heightening of all their longings had driven them both insane. They were crazy in each other's company.

She heard a tap on the door. She sat bolt upright and wiped the tears from her eyes.

'Come in,' she mumbled.

Mrs. McClennan opened the door. She had the papers piled high in front of her. 'I've brought you these, dear.' She looked at Hope's blotched and swollen face, her eyes bloodshot with tears. 'Whatever's the matter?'

She put the papers down on a chair and came over to Hope, putting her arm around her shoulder. Hope began to shudder with tears again.

'It's nothing . . . It's Craig. Everything's wrong between us.'

'Hush, now Hope. Don't fret. Craig needs time to work it all out. He didn't expect any of this to happen.'

'But I'll be gone in a few days.'

'That doesn't matter. Things will work themselves out between you two. Believe me.' She stroked her hand over Hope's shoulder. 'I'm not sure I've put any more weight on you girlie. You're still as thin as a rake. Now cheer up. I believe you're going out fishing with my family next?'

She was glad to have something to occupy her mind, physical work was a pain-blocker. Craig's image was imprinted on her mind, taunting and infinitely disturbing. Sometimes in the day, for a few moments she could block him out of her thoughts, but the nights were unbearable. At night there was nothing to take his image away and he haunted her until her dreams and waking thoughts were all obsessed with the same disturbing image.

The first two days of fishing were excellent. The sea was as calm as a mill-pond and Hope managed to collect good samples of mussels. But on the third day, when she walked down towards the quay in the early morning, the wind was blowing wild and blustery and she shivered beneath her coat. She remembered how Mrs. McClennan had talked to her the previous night.

'Craig phones me each evening to find out if you're back safely.'

'I'm safe enough with your husband and boys aren't I?'

'We none of us take the sea for granted. It can be very cruel. Very cruel. Every family on this island has lost someone to the sea at one time or another. Did you know that Craig's brother died at sea?' Hope shook her head. 'It was about this time of year. Eight years ago. A freak storm blew up and he was washed overboard. He was young, inexperienced, in the wrong place . . . his body was washed up at Grannad six days later.'

The colour ebbed from Hope's face. Now she understood why he hadn't wanted her to go fishing. Now she knew why he hated Grannad. All his feelings were locked up inside him and her heart wept for him.

As Hope approached Ian McClennan's boat, a gust of wind caught her and she had to steady herself before she continued. Ian walked towards her. He was a tall spare man and he wore a fawn bobble hat pulled down low over his head. She had no idea what colour his hair was, or whether he even had any.

'Hope. The wind's a bit strong this morning.

Are you sure you want to come out with us?'

'Will there be a storm?'

'Not according to the weather forecast. Not at the moment.'

'Will you be going out?'

'Yes.'

She needed the mussels. What if she didn't collect them and they were polluted? She'd never be able to forgive herself. 'I'll come out with you.'

The storm broke at about three. Until then the sky had been a bright blue. The wind had been blustery, but suddenly it changed direction and it started to howl in a tone that seemed ominous and cruel. The sky darkened to a blacky-grey. She had seen the sky like this before. She had watched a storm develop at Traisay one day, standing on the sand dunes, it had seemed dramatic and exciting. Out at sea it seemed treacherous and malignant and the waves now seemed full of venom and hatred. She had felt fear at Grannad; now she felt terror.

The wind gusted and waves broke over the sides of the fishing boat, tossing the vessel around as though it were a tiny piece of matchwood. She thought she'd feel sick, but she was too scared to feel sick, her body a tight knot of panic and screaming fear.

She remembered how Craig hadn't wanted her to go fishing, thought about how he had phoned every night to make sure she was safe.

He cared for her, she knew he cared for her and she loved him and if she ever saw him again she would tell him and have no fear of the consequences.

Her face was deathly pale as they slipped into harbour, out of the storm. Ian gave her a tot of brandy and pressed an arm around her. 'You're glad you're not a fisherman?'

She nodded, managing a wan smile. And she suddenly felt proud of herself. Proud that she had done everything that she had set out to do. Come what may, she could feel a sense of satisfaction in knowing that she had done all she could to help the fishermen.

Her legs were like jelly as she walked off the boat. She waved back to the McClennans and tramped doggedly along the quayside, her bucket of mussels in her hand. She stopped in her tracks. Someone was walking towards her. It was Craig. Her legs started to tremble, she was shaking all over. He stopped in front of her.

She moved towards him, dropping the bucket, putting her arms around him. He stood stiffly, unyielding, like a tin soldier on point duty, his body tight with unrelenting tension. She looked up at him and saw the muscles lightened like cords in his neck.

And then something in him seemed to snap and the life forged into his lean muscular body and he was holding her, nuzzling her, pressing her to him. 'Thank God you're safe,' he muttered throatily. 'I've been waiting here for hours, since I heard the storm warning. I thought . . .' and then his voice broke up and he pressed her face to his chest.

He was all-powerful and overwhelming and she knew she was nothing, felt nothing without him. And then suddenly, that knowledge bolted through her, sending cold alarm through her veins, frightening her. She was frightened of him, of herself, of where they were going. He kissed her and a wild trembling coursed through her and she opened her mouth to him knowing his feverish intent and then was shocked at the heat leaping in her loins; he was lighting a fire within her. But then the fright returned and she pulled away from him, shaking, her voice trembling.

'I got the mussels,' she said, trying to sound breezy and matter-of-fact.

He looked at her then, pain and contempt lacing his eyes. 'I think that's all you care about. Was it worth risking your life for?'

Something vital in him had snapped, she had wanted it to happen, but now her heart wept as she watched the remote mask drop over his face again. She could have spoken then, reassured him in soothing tones, told him of her love for him, but the panic was washing over her and she stayed silent and still, as though frozen in time.

He bundled her into the car, his movements were rough, almost uncoordinated. He sat down behind the wheel. He didn't start the car. He sat staring out of the windscreen, out across the harbour, so that Hope was reminded of the first time they met.

Suddenly the shock of it all—the storm, the waves, the thunderous noise of it all—seemed to whip around and catch her and before she knew it she was shaking with tears.

'I was frightened,' she admitted, her voice thin and shrill.

'I don't want to hear.'

'I thought about you.' She took a deep breath to steady her quivering lips and then smeared the tears away with a quick swipe.

'Haven't you got a handkerchief?' he barked. There was a frozen look to his face as though he had withdrawn to another time.

'No. I can't find it.'

A surge of defiance forced her to meet his eyes in subdued challenge, yet he had a pained haunted look to his face. His eyes had the bleakness of winter in them, shadowed by dark elements that instantly overwhelmed her and struck a quivering uncertainty in her heart.

He rummaged in his coat and produced a clean neatly folded square and he flung it at her and then he drove out of the harbour.

'Haven't you got anything to say?' she stammered.

'I said all I had to say before. Remember? I asked you not to go. But you . . . you don't care.'

183

'That's not true,' she wailed.

They reached the top of the hill. The car started its slow progress down towards the hotel and Hope felt a surge of joy at the beauty of the bay. No matter how many times she saw the bay, it always made her feel joyful.

'I love this bay.' She turned to him. He made no response. His face was a remote mask. She could see the tension in his neck, and his hands were bone-white, like tight cords, on the steering-wheel, with fine dark hairs silken on his wrist.

He stopped the car outside the hotel. They both got out. He put the bucket of mussels by the front door, hesitated and then walked back to the car.

'Aren't you coming in?' She had seen his hesitation and the look of despair in his eyes.

He turned to her then. His eyes full of contempt and something else she didn't understand, but it was something very important, she felt that.

'Tell Mrs. McClennan I'm going back to the cottage for a few more days.'

'I leave tomorrow.'

'Lucky you've been able to complete the survey,' he said contemptuously.

'Craig. We can't part like this. I need to talk to you.'

Hiding from herself was pointless now, the feelings were too strong, the love she felt too heady, something inside her was crying out for love, for passion, for the future, yearning for Craig. He looked at her, his eyes dark pebbles, as harsh as Grannad itself.

'I think we've said all there is to say.'

'No Craig. You're wrong. There's so much more to say. I was thinking about you all the time in that storm. Thinking about what I would say to you.' She moved close to him, taking his hands in hers. His were warm on her chilled skin and she shivered momentarily.

'Craig,' her voice had dropped to a low whisper, 'I love you.' She moved closer and stood on tip-toe, pressing a kiss to his sensuous lips.

'Have you been drinking?' he barked.

'Ian McClennan gave me a tot of brandy before, to steady my nerves.'

'I think he gave you more than a tot,' he carped sarcastically. 'Why don't you go in and take a nap? You'll feel much better when you wake up. Goodbye Hope. Safe journey tomorrow. You'll be glad to be home. You mark my words.'

CHAPTER FIFTEEN

But she wasn't glad to be back in London. She couldn't settle. It was as she had imagined.

The first thing she did was to talk to Roger. She told him that things could never be the way that he wanted and he had taken their parting with good grace. The next thing she did was to start applying for other jobs. She wanted to leave London, wanted to go anywhere where she could see the high open sky, hear the birds, listen to the wind through the trees, or see breakers on an open beach. London life, which up until now had excited her, now held no mysteries, like a party that had fizzed and lost its sparkle. And so like a deflated party-goer, she wanted to leave.

One Friday after work she took herself across the road from her flat to the tiny square, hoping to enjoy the dying rays of the sun as they filtered through trees and high buildings. It was an attractive square, a miniature park, with rhododendrons and azaleas in full bloom, all purples, vivid cerise and bright yellows. She sat down on an old iron bench, her eyes closed, listening to the blackbirds and sparrows in the silver birch trees, her thoughts travelling back to Branaigg.

Suddenly a shadow blocked out the sun. She opened her eyes and looked up. A man was standing in front of her. He was wearing light trousers, a fine striped white short-sleeved shirt, and carrying a jacket casually over one broad shoulder.

Hope bolted upright, her body tensing. She felt icy water flowing through her body. Feeling woke in her like a cold growling pain. She had tried to surround herself with a sterile lifeless vacuum but now, suddenly, feeling was rushing back and she knew she couldn't hold it back, and she said,

'It's you . . . what are you doing here . . . how did you find me?' The wave of cold washed over her, followed by a wave of heat and then she was terribly hot and shaky, her breath catching in her throat.

'Your flatmate, Ann, told me I'd find you here. I'm here because I have to talk to you.' He spoke in a flat tone that gave nothing away.

'I see. What do you want to talk to me about?'

'The island.'

Her heart sank. She knew her finished report had been published but somewhere inside she had ached for him to tell her he had come to talk about her, talk about them, and a secret part of her seemed to shrivel and die.

'Talk away,' she said, trying to keep a quaver out of her voice.

'Not here,' he insisted and before she knew what was happening he had scooped her up in his arms and was whisking her out of the park.

She struggled in his arms. In a flash of recollection that was more like a spasm of pain she was reminded of the strong lean feel of his body.

'Put me down,' she shrieked, but he tightened his hold on her.

'No. You're as light as a feather.'

'That's not the point. I don't want to be carried like this. I want—'

'You want. *You* want. I'm tired of hearing what you want. I'm doing what I want for once.'

Half luxuriating, half fearful, she let her head settle in the warm hollow between his neck and shoulders. Instinctively her hand went to the nape of his neck and she burned inside, need coiling in and around her, at the feel of his hair, silky, sensual, utterly erotic.

Outside her door he pressed the doorbell.

'I do have a key.'

'Keep it.'

Ann stood open-mouthed when she saw Hope and Craig. Without saying a word he stormed past Ann into the flat. Ann vacantly picked up her bag.

'I think I'll go and see Imogen. For a long chat.' The door closed behind Ann, and Craig dropped Hope carefully onto the sofa.

Hope's face was creased into a frown, her mouth pursed, she couldn't know how attractive she looked, but when she looked up Craig's glance ran over her appraisingly.

'What do you want?' she asked flatly.

'I've been to see the oil company today. Sir Gregory. Those other mussels were polluted weren't they? I wanted to thank you. Your doggedness paid off.' And then he added in a low throaty murmur, 'All those trips to the fishing grounds.'

Hope didn't speak, but her face started to burn with all the painful memories she had brought back from Branaigg. She looked up at him and glanced away hurriedly. He frightened her, breezing back into her life just when she had started to forget about him. There had actually been one fleeting moment today when he hadn't been uppermost in her thoughts.

'They've commissioned a thorough research project on the waters surrounding Branaigg. Sir Gregory's prepared to pay immediate compensation to the fishermen. And he's going to put some money into developing the fishing industry. I believe you suggested the area was suitable for oysters?'

She didn't speak. Words were beyond her. He stood before her, walking up and down the room in that graceful way of his.

'Sir Gregory wants you to go back to the island. Wants you to pave the way for the research group.'

'Whose idea was that?'

'His. I did inform him that you'd got on well with the islanders.'

'Most of the islanders,' she corrected him.

189

She stared at him. He was so gloriously attractive. She noticed the fine dark hairs tracing along his suntanned forearms. She'd never seen him wearing so few clothes. His presence tantalised her but she had to fight the spell he was weaving around her.

He was back. Trying to bulldoze her into doing something she didn't want to do. She didn't want to go back to the island, his island. She tried to put the skids on her emotions, tried to stop everything from whirring around her mind, but it was too late. It was like trying to stop a runaway train. Maybe it had been too late the moment she met Craig McAllister.

'You must come.'

'Must I?'

'Yes,' he stated emphatically.

'I don't think so. I'm applying for other jobs.'

'So I gather. The Lake District. Brecon Beacons. The Fens.'

'You've been doing your homework,' Hope quipped sarcastically.

'I needed to know what the opposition was.'

'The answer is still no.'

'Why? You told me yourself that you loved the island.'

'I wondered when that particular disclosure of mine would be thrown in my face.'

'What do you mean?'

'Didn't you ever notice? Anything I ever said seemed to be noted by you and distorted

190

and thrown back at me.' She'd been feeling defensive, quiet until now, but memories of their antagonistic battles started to flood back into her mind and she could feel the anger rising within her. 'I'd have to be a masochist to want to go back to Branaigg. That is . . . unless you decided to take up residence in . . .'

'Outer Mongolia?' he offered.

'Yes. Somewhere handy like that. Or perhaps the planet Venus.'

'Hope.' His voice had assumed those gentle soothing tones and she tried to turn her mind away from him. 'Hope. This is getting us nowhere.'

He sat down in the armchair, resting his hands over the ends of the arms so that they fell gracefully into mid-air. 'I have to talk to you.' He leaned across. His dark eyes gazing into her face.

'I need to explain why I've behaved so brutishly towards you.' He hesitated, his eyes reflective, as if he were somehow soaking her in and gathering his thoughts at the same time. 'You realise of course that I was convinced that you were another slick scientist totally uninterested in the fate of Branaigg and the livelihood of the fishermen. I even tried to convince myself that you were getting some special pay-off.'

He gave her a strange smile which made the delicate hairs on her skin stand straight up on end. 'It didn't take me long to see that you

191

were true and warm and honest and that your heart was in your work.'

'Is that why you kept telling me what a cold-hearted scientist I was?'

'I had to protect myself from you, any way I could. I couldn't afford to . . . to fall in love with you.' She turned away so that he wouldn't see that his words had made her suddenly feel rather hot.

'You asked me once if I had told you everything when I gave you my reasons for returning to the island.' She stared at him with wide green eyes. 'I didn't tell you all. I was badly hurt in a relationship with someone in the States. She deceived me. When she walked out on our relationship I was burnt out. Broken. I vowed I'd never get involved with anyone else again.

'And then you came along.' He leant over and gathered up her hand, sandwiching it between his own. Her skin seemed to burn under his touch, her breath caught in her throat and she felt her body trembling out of control. 'I had to block you out of my life, my thoughts. But somehow, God knows how, you'd managed to insinuate yourself into me. In here.' He pressed her hand to his chest, she felt his heart thundering beneath her fingertips and it was all she could do to keep control, to stop herself from falling, falling under his power. 'Do you understand what I'm saying?' he persisted softly, as if producing his voice in her blood, and she hardly heard his words at all.

Hope pursed her lips together, staring at him with wide shocked eyes and then he spoke again.

'Every time you got close I had to stop myself. I had to push you away. I had no choice. I had to protect myself. But it didn't work. When I went away you were still in my mind, in my dreams. I couldn't be free from you. And I found that the harder I tried to block you out the deeper you insinuated yourself into my . . . heart. You told me once you loved me, Hope. Now I'm telling you. I love you, Hope.'

'It was different then. *I* was different then. Things have changed Craig.' Using his first name made her feel uncomfortable. He made her feel uncomfortable, the way he stared at her with those deep dark eyes, staring as though looking into her very soul. She stood up and walked over to the window, looking out over the square, watching the trees rustle in the light breeze.

She felt him at her back. That sixth sense of hers warned her he was close, but she was not prepared for the soft heavy insistence of his voice.

'I love you Hope. I always have. I can't fight it any more. Fighting it didn't take the need away, didn't take the pain away.' He pressed his hands down on her shoulders, she wished he hadn't, her skin burned under his touch and she was falling, falling under his spell. Tension quivered through her in many layers, physical and mental and when he pressed a featherlight kiss to the sensitive lobe of her ear it snapped.

He pulled her around to face him. She was like a cornered bird, frightened and twitchy, her eyes wide, vivid and green. She looked away, looking anywhere but his face.

He pulled her chin up. 'Look at me,' he said softly and Hope felt the blood rushing through her body, her pulses thundering in her ears. He trusted her enough to cast aside the dark remote mask and let her see the naked passion, the impossible yearning beneath.

She pulled away defensively.

'I'll go now if you want.'

'Yes. Go,' she said, aware of a silly tremor in her voice.

'I'll go if you tell me that you don't love me.'

'I don't have to say anything.'

'I need to know.'

'Just go,' she said desperately.

He tilted her face up towards him, she felt his arm on her back spanning her slim waist. 'Tell me you don't love me and I'll go,' he insisted softly. He dropped his face on hers, a dark shadow over her face, and she tensed against him but he smothered the beginnings of her protest with his mouth, a very skilful mouth with a tongue that stroked and darted and made it seem as though she had just bitten into some exotic fruit of explosive sweetness. And then his arms closed tightly around her and she snaked her arms about his neck until she felt once more that fine silky hair at the nape of his neck and she groaned involuntarily.

He whipped his mouth away from her lips, plundering her neck and the lobe of her ear with kisses. 'Tell me you don't love me Hope.' His dark tones washed over her. 'Hope,' he repeated insistently and his voice turned her name into a caress and a light shiver ran over her skin. He sought her mouth again, his kisses deeper and more insistent.

She broke away from him and got out in a voice cracked with emotion, 'Go please. Go.'

'You don't love me?'

'I'm too frightened. I'm out of my depth.'

'Don't you think I know how you feel?' he said, putting all that strange softness into his voice as if he were stroking her with his words.

'I've been trying to forget about you,' she pleaded. 'And then you just breeze back into my life.'

'And have you?'

'Have I what?'

'Forgotten about me.'

'I managed to forget about you for ten seconds today. That's my all-time record.'

'Knowing you, you probably timed it.'

She stroked a finger along his cheek and smiled, softly, the sudden intensity of his gaze stirring all her pulse points. A mist rose before her eyes, hazing her vision along with her thoughts.

'You can't simply eradicate feelings by telling yourself you shouldn't have them. I know that now . . . and so do you. It's time we both stopped running away from our feelings, running away from each other.' He pressed his mouth firmly over hers. The kiss was tantalizing, tender, yet with a hint of controlled passion, and all the while his fingers were rubbing hypnotically against the fast pulse in her neck, soothing and yet inflaming her.

He seemed as though he were kissing her and holding her and loving her with great care, as though he had a fine edge to his passion, that he was afraid he might frighten her and that fear was controlling him. And she knew him then, totally, he was warm and honest and open and totally vulnerable and there was no going back, there never had been.

And then she no longer felt lost, confused, falling. Now she was home and she'd never felt so good.

'I've stopped running,' Hope managed as she snaked her arms about his neck, and, dissolving into a passion and intensity of feeling that welled up from a deep unknown source, she surrendered to his embrace.